# The VOYAGE of VAN ROUGE

## HEATHER SUMMERS

The right of Heather Summers to be identified as the
Author of the Work has been asserted by her in
accordance with the Copyright, Designs and
Patents Act 1988.

*The Voyage of Van Rouge* © Heather Summers 2020
https://heather-summers.my-online.store/
Illustrations © Pascale Cotasson (Paski)  2020

Edited by Shaun Russell
Editorial: Will Rees

Published by
Jelly Bean Books, Mackintosh House
136 Newport Road, Cardiff, CF24 1DJ
www.candyjarbooks.co.uk

ISBN: 978-1-913637-19-4

Printed and bound in the UK by
4edge, 22 Eldon Way, Hockley, Essex, SS5 4AD

*For Caleb & Layla with my love.*
*Be bold and follow your dreams.*

This is my first children's book and I can honestly say it has been a joy to write. I have many to thank for their support, and encouragement in helping me get this book on its journey beyond. Amongst others who have helped me along the way, I would particularly like to thank:

Hilary Ramsden for some of the inspiration for this book, a like-minded traveller and performer with whom I have shared many adventures over the years.

My daughters Sian Summers Issa and Meg Summers for the different ways they have assisted and supported me during this endeavour, not least the phonetic help from Sian for the many foreign words that appear throughout.

Katey Bass and the year three children of Claremont Primary School, London for their great feedback that is reflected in these pages; my fellow author friends Wollie Boehm, Biddy Wells and Sarah Green who have encouraged me as well as given me practical assistance.

Long time friend, Petra Schmidt who has encouraged me, listened and offered suggestions from the word go, and last, but crucially my talented friend, Pascale Cotasson (Paski) for her wonderful illustrations which are fun and joyful.

I cannot end without another big thank you to my editor and publisher, Shaun Russell of Jelly Bean Books for his enthusiasm, wisdom and support.

# – CHAPTER ONE –
## A MEETING, A WISH AND A VAN

*At the start of each chapter we will tell you how to say the foreign words that come up during that chapter and tell you what they mean. First you will see the foreign word, like the first Welsh word below (goch), then how it is pronounced (g-or-ch), then what it means (red). The sounds in CAPITALS show where the stress is. The words are in the order you will find them within the chapter.*

### A Stray Portuguese Word:
*Caramba!* = C-a-r-A-m-b-a = Gee!

### Welsh Words:
*Duw duw* = d-y-ew d-y-ew = oh my goodness.
In the next two words, say the *ch* as if you have a bad throat!
*Goch* = g-or-ch = red.
*Diolch yn fawr* = d-ee-O-l-**ch** u-n v-ou-r = thank you very much.

### French Words:
*Rouge* = r-oo-j-uh = red

*Vin* = *v-a* = wine

By the way, Van Gogh = *Van Goff*—he was a famous painter.

'Campervans, *Caramba*!'
Sweet P was over the moon to find the Welsh clifftop teeming with vans of all ages, sizes and colours. She dreamed of leaving her caravan in this lovely Welsh valley, cosy though it was, and setting off travelling in a campervan. Whenever she saw one parked up, she would try to peep through the window, then daydream it was her very own.

At this very moment she was surrounded by all types of vans. She chose the nearest one, peeped through the side window on tippy toes, and nearly fell over.

'Geez peas!' she cried. A funny face stared back at her. It had orange tufty hair and a red dot at the end of its nose. *It can't be my own reflection,* she thought. I have spiky, dark hair, a cute nose and rather large ears.

As she moved from camper to camper, she looked through the windows and found the same funny face looking back at her.. *Who is this?* she thought.

Quickly she ducked down and hurried to the next camper – a big yellow one with stripes down the bonnet. But this time she didn't look through **a** window. Instead she could see the orange tufty hair from behind. 'Got you!' she shouted, laughing.

'Indeed you have,' said the one with orange tufty hair as she turned to see her.

They both chuckled.

Sweet P fluttered her eyelashes, and the one with orange tufty hair wiggled her nose.

'Hi, I'm Sweet P. Do you love campervans too? I've always wanted one! It would be so great. I could then travel wherever I choose. Who are you anyway?' she said without taking a breath.

'I am Pumpkin, or you can call me Pumps for short, although I am actually quite tall.'

*You are rather round,* thought Sweet P, but decided not to say anything.

'I've been cycling around Wales, but I've worn out my bicycle. I'm not sure it will last much longer. I think it's broken.'

Pumpkin looked sad and pointed to the awful grey clouds. 'I'm also sick of the cold and rain. It would be great to jump in a van and go wherever the wind blows.'

Sweet P nodded in agreement. 'Does the wind blow to the Greek islands, do you think?' she asked.

'Funny you should say that.' Pumpkin scrambled through her bag and pulled out a book called *The Odyssey*. 'I've just been reading about ancient Greece.' She passed the book to Sweet P, who flicked through a few pages to be polite. 'It would be great to drive to Greece. Perhaps I could find a patch of land there to call my own. I've always wanted to grow tomatoes and chillies, and sit on a little chair in the sun.'

'Pumpkin, that sounds brilliant! ' A patch of land, right by the sea! I would go swimming every day.'

They high fived.

'We can only wish,' said Pumpkin, sighing.

Sweet P smiled dreamily. 'Actually, sometimes wishes do really work. Some people call it coincidence, but I believe if you want something that much—'

CRASH!

'Ouch!' she cried, rubbing her head. 'What was that?' Lying on the ground was a sign that had fallen off a tree and then bounced off her on the way down.

It read:

CAMPER VAN FREE
to GOOD HOME
CONVINCE ME
its YOURS!
KNOCK ON the DooR

'*Caramba!*' Sweet P shouted excitedly. 'This is it!'

'Hoodydoody!' cried Pumpkin in her orange-topped pumpkin voice.

They knocked loudly on the door by the tree.

'All right, all right,' said a large Welsh potato with black eyes, as he opened the creaky door.

'Well, *duw duw*, how can I help you two?'

'Hello, I'm Pumpkin.'

And I'm Sweet P. We'd really like to see your campervan please, mister.'

'Call me Spud. Of course you can see it, follow me.'

And there it was.

A big, shiny red van, with yellow curtains covered in stars, a sticker of a Welsh dragon stuck on the back, and a bicycle rack.

'Shame my bike is broken!' said Pumpkin.

They stepped inside and entered a tiny world of cupboards and sinks, as well as a sofa with plushy cushions, and a little table you could pop up and down.

'Wow, there's even an oven and a fridge,' said Sweet P as she excitedly opened the doors.

'And there's a wardrobe for our clothes,' said Pumpkin.

It was a little house on wheels with an engine, and although it was very old, it looked perfect for an adventure.

Sweet P quickly took her fiddle case from her back, whipped out her fiddle and began to play a jolly tune. Just like magic, Pumpkin pulled out a sparkly feather duster from under her jumper and gaily dusted whatever she could reach, finishing with Spud's large red nose.

'Ha ha, that tickles,' laughed Spud.

'Please let it be our camper, Spud!' said Sweet P.

'But why should I give you my big, shiny red van, Sweet P?'

'That's easy, we want to travel wherever the wind blows, and I'll play music along the way to make folk happy.'

'Tell me, Pumpkin, why should I give the big, shiny red van to you?'

'I want to make folk laugh on our journey,' said Pumpkin.

'*Duw duw*, you've both certainly made me laugh and happy. I'm a trumpet player, but I'm too old and stiff to travel where the wind blows. I no longer have enough puff to blow my own trumpet.' He stared down at Sweet P and Pumpkin. 'But how can tiny little things like you drive a big van like this?'

Sweet P stood on tippy toes to try to look taller. Her spiky hair bristled and her big smile was now an indignant 'O'.

'Pumps, can you drive this van?' asked Sweet P.

Pumpkin puffed out her chest. 'Yes, Sweet P, I can drive it. How about you?'

'Yes, I can!'

They both turned to Spud, defiantly. 'We can both drive this big van!'

Spud rubbed his bristly chin and scratched his grey baldy head. Sweet P and Pumpkin held their breath.

'*Duw duw*, I like your spirit. But there's also Turnip who wants it to carry her dogs around. Hmm, dogs, there'll be hairs over all these plushy cushions, and they'll scratch all this lovely woodwork. But she did come and ask me first. Hmm...'

Pumpkin and Sweet P exchanged a worried look.

'And we love speaking French,' said Pumpkin. 'If you give us the big red van we shall call it *Van Rouge*, won't we, Sweet P?'

'*Oh la la*, that's a great idea, Pumps.'

'I know, I'm full of them,' said Pumpkin proudly.

'Ha ha, I love *vin rouge*, red wine, you know,' said Spud. 'Well that decides the matter. I will give the van to you, Sweet P and Pumpkin. Please promise to look after it?'

'We promise!' they said together.

Sweet P smiled at Spud. It was the biggest, shiniest smile he had ever seen, and his eyes seemed to get even darker. Pumpkin punched the sky with joy and the red dot on her nose jumped up and down as they danced around *Van Rouge*, singing, 'Thank you, thank you, thank you, *diolch yn fawr*.'

Later, Spud waved them off, chuckling to himself at his own joke; he liked a nice painting by Van Gogh too. *Van Rouge* was also *Van Goch* and he liked them both.

# – CHAPTER TWO –
## READY SET GO!

*Welsh Word:*
Cwtch = *c-oo-ch* = a small cosy place.
* *GPS stands for Global Positioning System. Many smart phones have it to help you find your way somewhere. Although there is a difference between them, it's like a sat nav.*

'So, Pumpkin, which hand is the pebble in?' asked Sweet P as she held out her closed fists in front of her new friend.

'If you're correct you can choose who drives first.'

Pumpkin tapped softly on Sweet P's left hand, the one with the pebble.

'Er, um, I want you to drive first, Sweet P,' said Pumpkin.

Sweet P was secretly happy and Pumpkin was secretly relieved. Sweet P grabbed the keys and made her way to the front of *Van Rouge*.

'Thank goodness there's a step up,' said Sweet P, as she peered up at the large steering wheel. There was a big seat for two, roomy enough for both of them. Together they helped each other to climb up.

As Sweet P turned the key, *Van Rouge* roared into life.

'It's very noisy!' said Pumpkin.

'What did you say?'

'I said it's *VERY NOISY!*' shouted Pumpkin.

*Van Rouge* was also shaking, which made them feel quite dizzy. Slightly worried, Sweet P carefully drove out into the road. *Am I ready for this?* she thought, but soon remembered that she could do anything she wanted if she put her mind to it.

And that's exactly what she did.

'Sweet P, look at the beautiful flowers in the meadow. We can see so much from up here,' said Pumpkin in awe, looking through the giant windscreen.

'I feel like Queen P with the whole world stretched before me,' said Sweet P.

Back at Pumpkin's caravan, with *Van Rouge* safely parked up, they began to explore their new vehicle. The bumper was a bit wobbly and a headlight looked like it might fall off.

'I know what we need,' announced Sweet P, fetching a roll of black tape and carefully sticking pieces over all the wobbly bits.

With a loud screech, Pumpkin opened the wide sliding door on the side. 'Oh, I've got something to sort that out,' said Pumpkin. She reached into her huge rucksack that contained everything she owned.

'Some oil to put on it.' She squirted the oil on the hinges, and the noise stopped – for a short while anyway.

Inside, with the lights on and the starry curtains closed, it was *cwtch* cosy. Everything in this tiny home on wheels was made of wood. The walls and the ceiling were covered in woolly green cloth. The roof had two pop-up skylights.

Below this was a wardrobe with a big mirror. Pumpkin couldn't resist checking out her perfectly formed red dot on the end of her nose.

Once they'd finished exploring they sat down on the plushy sofa.

'Let's have a nice cup of tea,' said Pumpkin, as she headed towards the tiny kitchen at the back, followed closely by Sweet P.

Opening a cupboard, she found mugs and tea bags, and Sweet P found a kettle. Sweet P pressed a button on the sink and the water came out. They had everything they needed.

While they drank their tea, Pumpkin opened another cupboard.

'Oh, just look at all these lovely maps, Sweet P.'

Pumpkin loved maps. She liked to spend hours

looking at them, sticking them on tables, on chairs, on anything stickable really.

Sweet P liked maps too but she had to turn them upside down when navigating to be able to make sense of them. She was pleased to see that these maps were of mountains, and rivers, and seas, and maps of France, and Italy and...'

'Greece!' shouted Sweet P. 'This map tells us how to get to Greece!'

They studied the large map in fascination.

'Just look at all these islands. We have so much choice. I hope there's a ferry,' said Pumpkin.

'Let's check the map. Ah yes, we need to head to P-i-r-ae-u-s. It seems to be a big port near Athens. Isn't Athens the capital of Greece, Pumps?'

'Yes, I think so. We should go there and then choose which island to go to. We have a plan, Sweet P.'

They began to prepare *Van Rouge* for their big adventure. They packed all kinds of books about everything they might need to know. These included: *How To Drive A Van, Emergency Van Repairs, Maps Made Easy, How to Build a Tiny Home, How to Grow Chillies and Tomatoes,* and *Teach Yourself Greek.*

Pumpkin proudly put her GPS * at the front by the small sky windscreen.

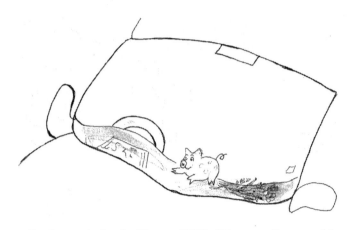

'It doesn't look like a GPS. It's a yellow rubber pig with blue spots!' exclaimed Sweet P.

'It's a Global Pig System – GPS, get it? If anyone drives badly we squeeze Pig and he will grunt at them loudly!'

They burst into laughter and could not stop for a while.

Once the giggling had finished, they packed *Van Rouge*. Sweet P packed her fiddle and compass. Pumpkin packed her juggling balls, red tutus, feather duster and cleaning brushes. Sweet P stowed paint pots, brushes and black sticky tape. Pumpkin put away tools and oil. They completed their list with toothbrushes, swimming gear and towels, a spare pair of knickers each, some clothes, and lots of food. They filled the shelves, the cupboards and cubbyholes. Everywhere was now full.

'We're ready to go, Pumps. It's a long way to

Dover, but if we leave now we can sleep during the crossing. Our ferry leaves at eight in the morning.'

'But, Sweet P, where's the bed? This sofa is plushy but it's small. There's only room for one of us.'

They looked under; they looked over; they looked upside down and downside up, but they could not find the bed. Then Sweet P had a brainwave.

'We've pushed and prodded, so let's pull. Come on... one, two, three! Ooch, you're squashing me. Get off, Pumpkin!'

They fell into a heap and just like magic the bed whooshed out from under the sofa. It was a bed big enough for two. They put sheets, pillows and a woolly blanket on top, and stored some bags and boxes underneath.

Outside it was now dark and wet. With a screech of the door, a roar of the engine, and a shake of everything else, they set off to Dover in the rain and wind.

It was midnight.

# – CHAPTER THREE –
## SCARY JOURNEY!

*Welsh Words:*
*Arafwch nawr! = a-r-AR-v-oo-ch n-ou-r* = Slow down
now! *(Remember that ch again – bad throat!)*
*Gofalys! = g-or-v-A-l-i-s* = Care!

As Pumpkin steered *Van Rouge* along the empty
road, she was finding it difficult to stay awake.
A flash of lightning made her jump slightly.
Pumpkin began to count, 'One potato, two potato,
three potato, four potato, five potato...' Distant
thunder rolled heavily through the heavens. *One mile
away*, she thought. Sweet P was still sleeping, even
with the rain lashing down.

Then there was another flash of lightning.

'Aargh!' shrieked Pumpkin as she swerved onto
the hard shoulder, avoiding the back of a lorry by a
whisker.

'Pumpkin, stop!' yelled Sweet P, who had been
shaken awake. Pumpkin switched off the engine.

'What is it, Sweet P, why are you shouting?'

'Didn't you see that lorry? You almost hit it.'

'No, I didn't. You must have been dreaming.'

'No, I'm fully awake. I know what I saw.'

For a second Pumpkin did not want to admit she was wrong, but she was sure her new friend would not lie. 'I'm tired, Sweet P,' she admitted. 'Can you drive now please?'

Sweet P nodded reassuringly, and tried to open the door. A gust of wind smashed it back into her. 'Ouch!' she cried.

Pumpkin moved over to Sweet P's seat and grabbed the door. Sweet P jumped out, but she was not looking where she was going. She did not notice an old tin lying by the side of the road. Pumpkin tried not to laugh when Sweet P tripped on it.

'Ouch, what was that?' cried Sweet P. She was once again lying in a heap on the ground, holding the tin in her hand. 'Just some litter.'

Pumpkin shook her orange tufty hair. 'No, it's actually quite nice. We'll have that!' said Pumpkin. 'We can use it to put plants in!'

Sweet P passed the tin to Pumpkin. Running against the rain and wind, she made her way to the driver's side. She tried to open the door but the wind was very strong. Eventually, with all the effort she could muster, she forced it open and swiftly climbed into the driver's seat, before it slammed shut.

'Urgh, you're soaking, get away from me!' said Pumpkin, as she stashed the tin under the seat with a bit of a shove and a push.

'It's all right for you. You're still warm and dry!'

Shivering, Sweet P switched on the engine and set off. It was still dark – no moon, no stars, no streetlights. They were driving along an extremely long motorway, with an incredibly great distance to go.

They hadn't even reached Swansea yet.

*Van Rouge* was shaking even more than before. Sweet P was finding this quite scary and nervously held on tight to the steering wheel. Thunder boomed and lightning flashed. It was a dark and treacherous night.

'La la, in my car, bla bla, it's so far. Drive this van? Yes I can!' sang Sweet P, or any old rubbish she could think of to keep herself awake.

Soon Pumpkin was snoring and Sweet P had to try very hard not to fall asleep herself. She didn't want to do exactly what she had accused Pumpkin of doing, so she stopped *Van Rouge* in a convenient lay-by and fell asleep instantly.

The wind howled, the rain beat down, the clock ticked on.

Sweet P cuddled up to Pumpkin.

'Get off me, Sweet P. I'm not a cushion! Look how

late it is. We'll miss the ferry if we keep on sleeping. Squeeze up, Sweet P, and swap sides so I can drive. I'm not getting out in this storm!'

It was awkward but it worked. Sweet P wished she had thought of doing the same thing herself.

When dawn finally broke, they were nearing Dover.

'Look, the ferry port is over there,' said Sweet P pointing at a sign. 'Pumps, go faster. It's nearly seven. They won't let us on if we're late.'

'I am going as fast as I can,' said Pumpkin, yawning.

It was just fast enough. At half past seven, they rolled onto the ferry a few seconds before the ramp clanked up.

By the time the ferry hooted – announcing its departure to Calais, France – Pumpkin and Sweet P were asleep outside, a shuddering heap on a long ferry seat.

If you happened to walk past all you would hear were snores and mutterings.

# – CHAPTER FOUR –
## OH LA LA, LA FRANCE!

*French Words:*
*Baguette* = *b-a-g-E-t* = type of French bread, stick shaped
*Patron* = *p-A-t-r-o-ng* (*but swallow the ng*) = boss
*Oh la la* = *oh la la* = well well, my goodness
*Merci* = *m-air-s-ee* = thank you
*C'était très bon* = *s-ai-t-ai t-r-e b-o-ng* (*but swallow that ng!*) = It was very good
*Oui* = *w-ee* = yes
*Prenez s'il vous plait!* = *p-r-U-n-ai s-ee-l v-oo p-l-ai!* = Please take!

'Drive right!' yelled Pumpkin.

'I *am* driving right. I think I'm driving quite well actually,' said Sweet P.

'No, I mean drive on the right. We're in France and they drive on the right here!'

Sweet P swerved to the right hand side of the road and stopped, just as a red car was fast approaching. She picked up the yellow, blue-spotted, rubber pig and squeezed a large grunt out of it as the car shot past.

'What are you doing that for? It wasn't that driver's fault, Sweet P. It was yours!'

Her heart racing, Sweet P was shaking after that near miss.

'Drive on the right, don't have a fright!' she said over and over again until it stayed in her brain. 'I think I need to eat.'

'A *baguette*!' cried Pumpkin.

'Get what bag? What are you on about?'

'Not a bag! A *baguette* is like a stick of bread. Look, there's *Café La France*. Perfect, let's stop here for breakfast. Get your fiddle, Sweet P.'

Sweet P loved her fiddle and she had been playing it for a long time. It felt like it was a part of her – like an extra arm. It was deep reddish brown, with lovely swirly f holes that let the sound out. It was a beautiful shape too, very curvy, a bit like Sweet P, who had a few curves herself. Every time she picked it up, she felt happy. Pumpkin checked her red dot and off they went.

Sweet P's French tunes went down very nicely while the café's customers were having their breakfast. The *patron* was pleased to have the chairs all dusted by a dancing Pumpkin with a red dot on her nose.

'*Oh la la, merci, c'etait tres bon*! We would like to offer you something to eat.'

They were very happy to sit down to *baguette* dripping with thick black jam, followed by a tasty croissant each. The tea was a bit weak and not so very hot, but they had heard that France wasn't really known for its tea. They left the café and walked through a leafy square with an old church.

'Wow, Pumps, look at that huge white bird sat in a nest on top of the steeple!'

'Isn't it a stalk, one of those birds you see in story books carrying babies in their beaks?'

They watched and marvelled until their necks were stiff from looking up at the sky and they could look no more. The delicious, warm smell of freshly baked *baguettes* and loaves of bread followed them all the way back to *Van Rouge*.

Back on the road they went. 'Drive on the right, don't have a fright!' chanted Sweet P at the wheel again.

Pumpkin read the map and gave directions. 'We want the next road on the right towards Chalons.'

After a few miles, Pumpkin said, 'Look, here it is, turn right.'

Slightly puzzled, Sweet P turned right. This is not what the sign said.

'What are you doing Sweet P? I said turn right!'

'I am turning right.'

'No you're not, you're turning left!'

'I'm turning right, Pumpkin, just like you asked me to do.'

'No, I didn't. Ah. Oh, yes I did... I was muddled up.' Pumpkin blushed, she didn't like to be wrong.

In the rolling countryside there were red poppies everywhere; in the fields and by the side of the road as far as they could see. There were so many growing they thought it would be fine to pick a few, so they stopped and gathered a posy. They put them in a small tin of water and propped them up by the small sky windscreen and Pig.

A big lorry came around the bend in a terrible hurry and passed so close that *Van Rouge* shook. Pumpkin was very quick to squeeze several grunts from Pig.

'*Oh la la,*' she tutted, 'that was close!'

'"*Oh la la*" is a bit like "*duw duw*" in Welsh, or "oh my goodness" in English, isn't it?'

'*Oui,*' said Pumpkin.

'What do you mean, wee? Do you need one?'

'No, I mean yes, you twit!'

'Well this is all very confusing,' muttered Sweet P, not happy at being called a twit.

Soon it was Pumpkin's turn to drive, so Sweet P picked up the map and turned it upside down, so that it was pointing in the direction they were going. She sang quietly as she studied it.

After driving for a while, Pumpkin stopped suddenly.

'Look at all those bricks in a pile. See the sign by them? "*Prenez s'il vous plait!*" We're going to need to build a little home on our tiny patch of land, so let's have them!'

'But where are we going to put them, Pumpkin?'

'Why, under the bed of course!'

Sweet P groaned. 'But there's loads of things under the bed already!'

'We can soon change that Sweet P!'

They moved the bags and boxes onto the bed and piled the bricks neatly underneath, so that they would all fit in. After a great deal of effort they were hungry.

They spread out their blue and white checked rug on the grass and prepared a delicious picnic of *baguette*, yellow cheese and tiny tomatoes, all washed down with apple juice. It was a lovely blue sky day, so they lay down for a little doze amongst the red poppies.

# – CHAPTER FIVE –
## BEANS, BOULES AND STUFF

*French Words:*
*Mesdemoiselles* = *m-ai-d-e-m-w-a-z-E-l* = young girls/women
Now remember to swallow the <u>ng</u> in the next two and the last one
*Non* = *n-o-<u>ng</u>* = no
*Bonsoir* = *b-o-<u>ng</u>-s-w-AR (rhymes with car)* = Good evening
*Boules* = *b-oo-l* = bowls, but a different game to English bowls
*Au revoir* = *oa r-u-v-w-AR (rhymes with car)* = Goodbye
*Cocorico* = *c-o-c-o-r-i-c-OA* = cock a doodle do
Pardon = *p-ar—d-o-<u>ng</u>* = sorry

They awoke an hour later, excited to get going again. It was early evening and there weren't very many cars on the road, so they drove for a little while through the empty French countryside.

'Look, Pumpkin, let's stop and see what those French beans are doing over there.'

Each bean was holding two silver balls. They were taking it in turns to roll them on the ground. The winner was the ball closest to the target, a tiny silver ball that was rolled first.

'*Bonsoir, mesdemoiselles,* you want to try?' asked a young, fresh-faced bean, offering them each a silver ball.

'*Bonsoir* and *merci!*' said Sweet P, smiling.

'It's heavy,' said Pumpkin, picking up a ball.

'The game is *boules,*' said a tall, thin bean with a moustache, and wearing a beret and a pair of round spectacles. Pumpkin and Sweet P each rolled their *boule*.

'Not bad, Pumps!'

Sweet P rolled another *boule*, but it went in the opposite direction, disappearing out of sight. They played another game and lost, but it was great fun to play. An old grey bean in a green cloth cap won.

'It that your van?' asked the old grey bean, after the game.

Pumpkin and Sweet P nodded.

'It's very old, *non*? Where can you go in this?'

'We're going to Greece,' said Pumpkin, crisply.

She had not said anything funny, but the beans started to laugh. Pah, they were laughing at *Van Rouge*. How dare they?

'I think it does not go to Greece, *mesdemoiselles*, ha ha ha! Look, it is breaking,' he said, pointing at the sticky tape and a few dents. The small hole in the door appeared suddenly bigger.

'How rude! We've come a long way from West Wales, Mister Bean, and we plan to drive all the way to Greece,' replied Sweet P, miffed.

'*Merci* and *au revoir*, let's go, Sweet P!' Pumpkin stomped off, closely followed by Sweet P.

They were slightly disgruntled and getting tired and hungry. Soon they found a lovely grassy place to stop for the night. It was by a lock on a canal. They heated up a can of soup, and ate it with yellow cheese and *baguette*, followed by French cherries.

'Bedtime?' suggested Pumpkin.

They couldn't see the bed for boxes and bags. In

30

what would become a nightly routine on their journey, they moved everything off the bed onto the seats in the driver's cab. They closed the starry curtains, cleaned their teeth and went to sleep.

The light of the waxing moon twinkled on the water, a barn owl hooted and the night hours ticked by.

Suddenly the peace was shattered. '*Cocorico!*' called a cockerel over and over again.

Then 'Ding Dong' chimed the nearby church bells over and over again.

'What's going on?' cried Sweet P, as she shot bolt upright in bed.

'It's too early!' moaned Pumpkin, groggily reaching for the clock. It said seven o'clock.

They dragged themselves out of bed. It was very warm already, so they pushed open the pop-up skylights in the roof. Then they made a nice cup of tea. Sweet P had her large bowl of muesli. Pumpkin dipped her plain biscuits into her tea, and then had a hard-boiled egg.

It was lovely sitting by the water in the early sunshine. 'Look at the canal boat, Pumpkin!' They waved to a round, friendly-looking pea with frizzy hair who was driving the boat. A skinny bean, with a long beard, was hanging out some clothes to dry on a short washing line. They both waved back. It was fascinating watching them pass through the lock.

'I wonder if we'll get anywhere near Switzerland today,' mused Pumpkin as she looked at the map. 'There are lots of lines close together where it says 'Alps' and some big numbers. I wonder if that's the height of the mountains. One number is 3328. Wow, I think it's going to get very hilly!'

An hour later, they set off with Pumpkin at the wheel.

A fast car drove towards them on the wrong side of the road, then swerved, blasting them with their horn.

'Take that and that!' shouted Sweet P, grunting Pig loudly out of the open window.

'He was going too fast to hear that, the dingbat!' said Pumpkin, as they drove through the cobbled streets of a French town. It appeared to be outdoor market day.

'Let's check the market out,' said Sweet P.

Pumpkin agreed, and they parked *Van Rouge* on the side of the road.

The market looked amazing. There were stalls selling fruit and vegetables, farm cheeses, colourful clothes, wooden toys and painted cups and mugs, tools, secondhand books, garden plants, wine, honey, flowers, homemade bread, eggs and much more. It was dazzling. There were folk everywhere, chatting to their friends and to stallholders, filling their bags and baskets with all sorts of delights.

'What a buzzy place. I love it,' said Sweet P. 'Shall we do a bit of busking and see what happens?'

They quickly grabbed Sweet P's fiddle from *Van Rouge*, as well as tutus and juggling balls. Pumpkin laid an old bowler hat on the pavement and threw a few coins into it.

'Shouldn't it be our audience putting money into the hat, Pumps?'

'People will think we've already had an audience and they like what we're doing. It's just to give folk the right idea!'

Before long they had attracted a crowd, and coins of different sizes were flying into the bowler hat. Sweet P played some French tunes as well as Welsh ones, and folk were dancing arm in arm, twirling around each other.

'Woah!' cried Pumpkin, as one couple fell into her and knocked her juggling balls flying.

'*Oh la la, pardon,*' said the stringy leek as he threw a handful of coins into the hat.

'That's OK. I guess it was worth nearly being knocked over,' Pumpkin said, laughing. 'Shall we go and spend all this money?'

A local farmer had a rabbit for sale and Pumpkin looked at it longingly.

'Um, Sweet P, do you—'

'No, Pumps, don't even think about it!'

'Too late, I already am!'

'OK, thinking about it is fine, but stop right there! In Greece we could get a rabbit, but not yet. Besides, wouldn't it eat our veggies? I'd rather get chicks like those weeny ones over there. Chicks grow into chickens, and chickens lay eggs.'

'Good point! Those chicks it is then.'

'Oh, Pumpkin, be serious, how can we have them in *Van Rouge*? We'd lose them in there, and they would poo everywhere! But when we get our tiny patch of land we could get some then.'

'Oh, all right, but let's get some eggs anyway, and honey—'

'And cheese, tomatoes, strawberries and cherries,' added Sweet P.

Turning around they noticed a bread stall.

'And *baguettes*!' they said at the same time, bursting out laughing.

Laden with their goodies, and half of the euros spent, they tried to find spaces in *Van Rouge* to store it all.

It was difficult, but soon they were back on the road. They rounded a bend and saw a mountain of pallets lying by the roadside. It looked as though they had been there for a long time. Grass was starting to grow up between them.

'Wow, look at those, Sweet P. Think of the furniture we can make for our tiny house: seats and tables, even a sofa, if we put some cushions on top.'

'On no, you've got to be kidding, Pumps! There is no way we can fit them in. The bed is already full underneath and on top it's covered in bags and boxes!'

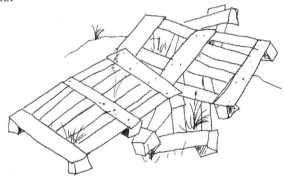

But Pumpkin would not be deterred.

'Look, Sweet P. We can put them under the mattress. You'd never know they were there.'

'Mmm, but they're filthy,' said Sweet P, crossing her arms.

'That's OK. I can clean them with my brushes.'

Sweet P sighed and half-heartedly helped take everything off the bed. They loaded in four pallets, laying them flat like a jigsaw. Once this was done, they put the mattress and everything else back on top.

Pumpkin climbed up and pretended to sleep. Sweet P climbed up and hit her head with a bang!

'Ouch, we're very close to the roof, you know.'

'It's a great view from here, Sweet P. You'll get used to it!

'I suppose so,' said Sweet P, rubbing her sore head. 'We are using things that people don't want.'

'It would only rot away. We're doing our thing for the environment,' said Pumpkin.

'Well said, Pumps. But that's it! We don't have any more space, not for anything else.'

Pumpkin remained silent.

It was dark when they stopped for the night, somewhere in France close to the Swiss border. They were very high up when they went to bed. Getting up for a wee in the night was quite tricky.

# – CHAPTER SIX –

## SMOKING BRAKES AND SNOWBALLS

*Italian Words:*
*Meccanico = m-e-c-A-n-i-c-o* = mechanic
*Grazie = g-r-A-t-s-ee-e* = thank you
*Buongiorno = b-w-o-n-j-OR-n-oa (rhymes with 'go')* =
Good morning
*Signorine = s-i-ng-y-or-EE-n-e* = misses or young
women
*Diamine! = d-ee-AR-m-i-n-e* = Oh heck!

'What are those tinkling sounds?' murmured
Sweet P, sleepily.
She climbed down and opened
the ever-screeching sliding door.
There was a herd of black and
white cows staring at her, all
with metal cowbells hanging
around their necks.

The Alps were rising up in the near distance.
Some of them looked as if they were wearing white
caps.

'Look, snow, Pumpkin, in May! That's incredible! It feels so warm.'

'It must be very cold so high up, I guess,' said Pumpkin.

'Don't the mountains look beautiful?' said Sweet P, completely delighted.

Pumpkin nodded, unfolded the map and pointed. 'We need to find the Saint Gotthard Pass.'

Sweet P glanced over Pumpkin's shoulder at the map. 'The roads look ever so bendy,' she said.

Soon they arrived at the border with Switzerland, where they had to stop.

'Please open your doors,' said the border guard, a serious-looking carrot with a pointy face. Pumpkin set out the folding chairs, so that she and Sweet P could wait in comfort, while the guards searched *Van Rouge*.

'Cup of tea, Sweet P?'

'No thanks. What are they looking for, do you think?' asked Sweet P. 'Treasure?'

'Maybe a stowaway!' said Pumpkin.

The guards looked in disbelief at all the bags, boxes, bricks and pallets.

'Thank you, that's all,' said serious-looking carrot, rather grumpily.

As quickly as they could, they packed away their tea things, as well as their folded chairs, and swiftly drove away.

As soon as they reached a safe distance, they burst into fits of laughter.

'Ha ha ha! I'm sure they didn't expect all this stuff,' said Pumpkin.

'What kind of stowaway?' mused Sweet P. 'A smuggler, or someone who has no money for a ticket, do you think?'

Pumpkin pondered. 'There are wars and fighting going on. Some folk are forced to run away when it's too scary to stay in their own country.'

'To a safer country, I suppose,' said Sweet P. 'If we find a stowaway, should we hide them? There's not exactly any room left.'

Pumpkin did not answer. She was busy looking at wooden chalets, with painted shutters and balconies. 'Look at the huge log piles neatly stacked by each house. I guess they light a lot of fires around here. It must get very cold,' said Pumpkin.

'We can see snow on some mountaintops in spring, so there's probably a lot of snow everywhere in winter. Those roofs are very deep. Look how steeply they slope. Wow, imagine sledging down those, Pumps!'

'I think the snow would actually slide off before you could do it. Turn left here, Sweet P.'

'I think you mean right, Pumpkin. Left would take us into the bank,' she said, turning right.

Pumpkin blushed and went very quiet. She didn't like to be wrong. It was obvious that her rights and lefts were muddled up. *It's because we're driving on the opposite side of the road*, thought Pumpkin.

Minutes later, they drove into a charming village. In the central square was a beautiful old stone fountain. It was in the shape of a frog and had water spouting from its mouth.

They quickly parked up *Van Rouge* and skipped over to the fountain. Sweet P took several deep gulps. She loved drinking water. 'Wow, this water is delicious, try it,' she said.

'It's our pride and joy, spring water straight from the mountains,' said a passing parsnip with a jaunty spring in his step.

'No wonder it tastes so good!' cried Sweet P.

Sensibly they filled their water bottles and water carriers. The tasty water would keep them going for a while.

Half an hour later, they drove on a busy road leading to the Pass. Soon they came to the mountain. They put their lights on as they headed underground.

'What a long tunnel!' exclaimed Pumpkin.

It seemed to go on forever.

And a little longer than that.

Then, all of a sudden, they could see daylight approaching and they were out in the bright sunshine.

But, before they knew it, there was another tunnel.

And another.

Some tunnels had big windows and you could see a streak of mountain flash past.

Others were dark and scary.

As they drove into sunlight, Sweet P was surprised to see smoke. 'Oh, Pumpkin, we're smoking!'

'What do you mean we're smoking? I most certainly am not and please don't, Sweet P!'

'I mean *Van Rouge* is smoking, look!'

Clouds of smoke were billowing out in front of them and *Van Rouge* did not smell right.

They stopped and opened the bonnet. It was steam, not smoke.

'I think our water level is too low,' said Pumpkin.

'Ouch, the radiator is really hot!' said Sweet P, sucking her burned finger.

Pumpkin grabbed a flask full of water and began unscrewing the radiator cap. It started spluttering and spitting hot water.

'Stop, Pumpkin! You'll get sprayed with boiling water! We have to let *Van Rouge* cool down first.'

'While we have a nice cup of tea,' said Pumpkin.

They took their time over their cup of tea to make

sure *Van Rouge* had really cooled down before they filled the radiator.

Soon they were driving on the road that led directly to the Pass. *Van Rouge* started climbing, but was very slow. The road was getting extremely steep with many tight bends. Poor *Van Rouge* was finding it difficult to climb.

The bends became more and more twisty. *Ah, I get what a hairpin bend is now. They bend back on themselves just like hairpins do*, thought Sweet P.

As they crawled up the hill, the line of cars behind them grew longer. They felt slightly guilty, but there was nowhere to pull off on this steep and narrow road.

'Uh oh, what's that strange sound? Sounds like something is rubbing! Can you hear it, Pumps?' Sweet P was tuned into the sound of *Van Rouge* in the same way she was tuned into the sound of her fiddle. Something caught the corner of her eye through her side window. 'On no, there's more smoke coming from somewhere else at the front!'

'Look, Sweet P, we're almost at the top. We can stop at that lay-by over there,' said Pumpkin. 'There must be something else wrong with *Van Rouge!*'

All the cars that were behind them drove past, their occupants staring hard at them.

Once *Van Rouge* was parked, they forgot their

troubles as they leaped out and jumped into a small white carpet of wonderful snow. Their whoops of delight echoed around the mountains. Pumpkin made three snowballs and juggled them expertly.

Sweet P wasn't the best juggler, but having tried and failed, she kept one snowball in her hand.

'Wow, that's great, Pumpkin, and so is this!'

PLOP!

A large snowball landed on Pumpkin's head. It trickled down her neck, as she danced around, trying to get it out.

'Eek! That's cold and wet! Right, I'll get you, Sweet P!'

The air was soon full of flying snowballs, some finding their mark, others whizzing pitifully off course. They laughed so hard, and then fell into a soft pile of snow and looked up at the big, blue sky. Sweet P gazed at the mountains. 'Wow, what a view, Pumps. It's fantastic!'

Sparkling snowflakes twinkled in the nooks and crannies in the rocks. Something else twinkled and caught Pumpkin's attention. She started digging with her hands into the cold, crisp snow.

'Wow, look at this. It's a bell, like the ones hanging around the cows' necks. A cow must have lost it!'

'It will make a great doorbell, Pumpkin. Good find! And it's small too, phew!'

'Look!' said Pumpkin, the smell of smoke a sudden reality check. 'There's the smoke, it's coming from the driver's wheel! We need to find help soon or we won't ever get to Greece. Let's get going Sweet P? *Van Rouge* can roll down the mountain from here!'

'Yes, let's do it!'

They jumped aboard, Pumpkin into the driver's seat.

Sweet P affectionately patted *Van Rouge's* dashboard. 'Come along, girl. You can do it.'

Down...

Down...

Down...

Into the valley they rolled, with smoke billowing out.

At the bottom they stopped by the roadside to find other vehicles parked up as well. They pulled out the *Emergency Van Repairs* book and found the page *Trouble Shooting.*

Following instructions they tried to push *Van Rouge* to see if it would move.

It wouldn't.

'It must be the brake then, Pumpkin.'

They were so absorbed in their task that they didn't hear approaching footsteps.

'*Buongiorno, signorine*, I am Paulo, *meccanico*. You are having a problem? Can I help you?' said a smiling Italian turnip, with kind eyes and black, springy hair. He was wearing overalls and big boots.

'Oh, hello, yes please. We have a big problem!' said Sweet P.

They all pushed *Van Rouge*, but it would not budge and Paulo looked at the smoking wheel.

'Ouch, it's hot!' Sweet P sucked her finger, the same one she had already burned on the radiator.

'I can do nothing here, but if you drive very slowly to my garage, I will mend it for you. It is in Bellinzona, please follow me.'

They followed Paulo's van, but after a little way he stopped in a lay-by.

'*Oh diamine*, now my van breaks down! I must leave it here. I will come later for it. I come with you, I drive, *si*?'

And so Paulo drove them in *Van Rouge* to his garage about forty minutes away. Pumpkin sat in the middle, Sweet P by the window.

'Hey, careful!' yelled Sweet P, as Paulo nearly drove them into an oncoming car.

'So sorry, the steering wheel it is on the wrong side!' said Paulo with a laugh. Sweet P did not find it at all amusing.

At the garage Paulo put *Van Rouge* on a ramp to have a look.

'As I was thinking, it is the brake sticking. It needs a new brake.'

'I thought I heard something rubbing!' cried Sweet P.

'I can mend it tomorrow,' said Paulo. 'You sleep here on the ramp and I come in the morning to fix it. OK?'

'Um yes, *grazie*, Paulo. We'll look after your garage. See you in the morning!' said Pumpkin.

'Bye, *grazie*,' called Sweet P.

The garage was a bit dirty, so they got out the cleaning brushes and made the garage sparkly clean – well a bit cleaner anyway. Pumpkin gave *Van Rouge* a quick whizz with her feather duster.

Then it was time for dinner. They made a cheese omelette in a *baguette* and followed this by munching a few fresh strawberries. It was all from the market.

At bedtime, they climbed up the steps, onto the ramp, up very high to the top of their bed.

'Don't look down or you'll get dizzy, Sweet P.'
Sleep came quickly and oh so sweetly.

# – CHAPTER SEVEN –
## A STORM AND A WETTING

**Italian Words:**
*Signorina* = *s-i-n-g-y-o-r-EE-n-a* = miss or young
lady
*Addio* = *a-d-EE-oh* = goodbye
*Lago* = *l-AR-go* = lake
*Maggiore* = *m-a-j-OR-ai* = greater

Sweet P and Pumpkin must have been very tired
when the following morning Paulo called out,
'*Buongiorno signorine*! You still sleeping?'

Sweet P bounced out of bed, forgetting about the
ramp. 'Oo, ouch, what happened?!'
she cried as she tumbled
to the floor.

'Oh, *signorina*! You are
OK?'

Sweet P continued to moan
and groan. 'Just a bit sore and slightly
embarrassed. I'm wide awake now though!' She
staggered to her feet, a little dazed and wobbly.

Pumpkin came to the rescue with a spot of

breakfast, and a nice cup of tea for everyone.

Then she helped Paulo by passing him the tools he needed to fix the brake. While this was happening, Sweet P removed her fiddle from its case and played a jolly Italian tune. Paulo beamed happily, while Pumpkin couldn't resist making a few twirls with her feather duster.

'Ah, this is why my garage is now so clean!' said Paulo. '*Grazie!*'

Half an hour later, with the brake finally mended, Paulo appeared to have something on his mind. He pulled one of his springy curls. 'You can help me?' he asked.

Sweet P nodded. 'One good turn deserves another.'

Paulo held up two wooden poles, each one over two metres long. 'See these poles, I do not want them. Please take them to the recycling in your van.'

Sweet P and Pumpkin exchanged a glance and nodded in agreement. 'Yes, of course,' said Pumpkin grinning. 'Can we keep them instead, please, Paulo?'

'Oh no!' groaned Sweet P, who crossed her arms. She looked slightly fed up with Pumpkin.

Paulo seemed rather surprised. 'Of course, but why, *signorina*?'

Before Sweet P could say anything, Pumpkin loaded the two poles into the back of *Van Rouge*.

'I have a plan, Sweet P,' said Pumpkin, producing some rope. 'We can hang them above the bed. They can be our washing lines, well, washing poles!'

'But... oh, OK,' said Sweet P. 'That actually might come in handy, especially for drying our swimming costumes when we're driving along.'

Loaded up, they waved goodbye and set off for the Italian lakes.

'Bye, Paulo, *grazie!*' they called.

'*Addio signorine! Grazie* from Paulo!'

'*Lago Maggiore*, here we come!' announced Sweet P, grinning from ear to ear.

They drove the short distance from the town to a beautiful lake, surrounded by mountains on all sides. They made their way slowly along the lakeshore and admired the flowers in the gardens. It looked like a scene out of a picture book. After a while the sun disappeared.

'Oh no, the weather is changing,' said Pumpkin, pointing to the mountains. 'I don't like the look of those black clouds. I think they might be coming our way, Sweet P!' They certainly looked ominous.

'We'd better shut the skylights before it rains.' Sweet P pulled over in a lay-by overlooking the lake. They watched the black clouds roll in. It was very dramatic.

Twenty minutes later, they jumped into the back of *Van Rouge* to close the skylights.

'Um, Sweet P...'

'Yes?'

'Where are the skylights?' asked Pumpkin, pointing at two big holes where the skylights used to be.

'Oh no, they must have blown off while we were driving,' said Sweet P. At that very moment lightning split the sky.

'One potato, two potato.'

'What are you doing, Pumps?'

'Ssh! Three potato, four potato.' And thunder cracked dramatically! 'Four seconds.'

'What do you mean, four seconds?' asked Sweet P.

'Oh, Sweet P, this is really cool. If you see a flash of lighting, count until you hear the thunder. It is five seconds for every mile. And if thunder and lightning happen at the same time, it means we're in the centre of the storm.'

'OK, does that means that we're less than a mile away?' asked Sweet P.

'That's right,' replied Pumpkin.

And then, plop, a fat drop of rain dripped on Pumpkin's red dot, another on Sweet P's big ear. Then plop, plop, plop came more drops thick and fast.

Pumpkin grabbed some sticky tape and two big plastic tablemats. 'I'm going on the roof to tape up the holes.'

'With tablemats?'

'Yes, unless you've got a better idea.' Pumpkin leaped out of *Van Rouge* and started climbing up the bike rack. As she precariously climbed, the sky flashed brightly, lighting up her body against the dark night sky. At the same moment thunder crashed, then rumbled. It was like a giant rolling a piano across the heavens.

'I'm sure the tarpaulin's here!' yelled Sweet P, as she pulled everything out from their cubbyholes.

She looked into sky. It was now raining heavily and the inside of *Van Rouge* was getting soaked. It was like a thousand taps had been turned on all at once.

'Help me, quick!' yelled Pumpkin, banging on the roof to make herself heard through the noisy rain.

'Found it!' Sweet P jumped out of *Van Rouge*, and unceremoniously fell face first into the mud. She picked herself up, pushing forward against the rain and the wind. As her muddy hands climbed up the bike rack, she threw the tarpaulin at Pumpkin. Pumpkin caught it, but almost slipped when she tried to fasten it to the roof.

Job done and wet through, they dived back inside and grabbed towels to dry themselves.

'You've stopped the rain coming in, Pumps. Fantastic!'

Pumpkin looked pleased. She liked to do well.

Wrapped in towels, they looked out of the windscreen. The wipers were ferociously swishing backwards and forwards as the thin lightning forks illuminated the lake. At the same moment, thunder burst, rolled and echoed around the Alps. It was quite amazing; the storm was now directly overhead. They watched in awe as the lightning targeted the mountains, and a few unfortunate trees.

Once the storm was over, they changed into dry

clothes and decided to take a walk by the lake. Twinkling lights blinked along the shoreline and a big yellow moon appeared from behind the clouds.

'Oh, it's so beautiful. Let's stay here tonight. We can swim in the lake in the morning,' said Sweet P.

And that's what they did.

They heated up lentil soup on their tiny stove and treated themselves to hot cocoa before bedtime.

# – CHAPTER EIGHT –
## A PICKLE AND GELATO

*Italian Words:*
In both of the following 'oa' rhymes with 'go'
*Gelato = j-e-l-AH-t-oa* = ice cream
*Molto bene = m-O-l-t-oa  b-e-n-e* = very good

Pumpkin and Sweet P awoke to brilliant sunshine. They removed the tarpaulin from the roof, so that everything could dry out, and draped it over a picnic bench to dry.

'What's the chance of finding a pair of pop-up skylights along the road, Pumpkin?'

'Not sure, but you never know.'

After tasty eggy bread and tea, they quickly washed up and changed into their swimming costumes. As they walked into the lake, a mother duck and her five ducklings glided quietly past.

Sweet P always liked to dive into the sea, but somehow lakes made her feel more cautious, possibly because lakebeds are often muddy and weedy.

'Wow, it's c-c-cold water!' cried Pumpkin as she paddled in, not sure whether she would actually swim.

Sweet P had waded in on tiptoes to where it was deeper. 'Last one in does the washing up!' she called, as she plunged into the water, swimming around and around, saying, 'It's actually quite warm after a bit!'

'Pah, I don't believe you!' Pumpkin tried to swim a few strokes backwards and forwards, before quickly getting out again. 'I wasn't ready when you made that call. It's still your turn to wash up, Sweet P.'

Back in *Van Rouge*, after washing up (who do you think did it?) and packing everything away, Pumpkin drove them along the lake's edge. It was so narrow – the lake on one side, the steep mountainside on the other. There was also a lot of traffic. They passed through many small, quaint towns, and it was becoming hot again. Pumpkin was desperate to stop.

'I'm going to look for somewhere to park. I need a *gelato*. That's scrummy Italian ice cream.'

'I know that,' said Sweet P indignantly.

Instantly Pumpkin turned down a cobbled street, a very narrow one.

'Oh, Pumps, it's one way. Look, all the cars are coming towards us. None are going our way, and there are a lot of angry faces!'

Horns blared at them, folk stared at them, and drivers shook their fists. What a pickle they were in.

'Quick, you drive, Sweet P, I'll direct the traffic.'

'But you got us into this mess, Pumpkin. You get us out of it!'

Sweet P had no choice but to get into the driver's seat as Pumpkin grabbed her cleaning brushes. She checked her red dot and put on her fluffy red tutus – one on her head and one around her waist.

Soon she was directing the traffic with her brushes.

Miraculously, turnip, asparagus and zucchini folk of all ages, shapes and sizes started to laugh. Young beans were running up and down in excitement. The street was full of folk laughing as well as cars hooting to join in the fun. Sweet P could not move *Van Rouge* a single centimetre. Finally, after Pumpkin's bold directions, Sweet P reversed back up the narrow street. It was very tricky and she was sweating profusely.

Pumpkin gave her a quick dust with her feather duster to cool her down. 'Stop it, Pumps! I need a *gelato* after all that hot work,' said Sweet P, who was changing into a tutu and grabbing her fiddle from its case. Pumpkin checked her red dot and picked up her juggling balls. They soon found a perfect *gelato* café in the square, where Pumpkin could juggle to Sweet P's lively Italian tunes. After a while, she ran out of those. 'OK, time for some Welsh tunes!' cried Sweet P.

As her jigs and reels got faster, so did Pumpkin's juggling. It went down very well with everyone in the café. Exhausted, Pumpkin and Sweet P finally plonked themselves down, just as a smiling waitress – a cute radish – came over.

'*Molto bene, grazie!* We offer you *gelato, si?*'

'Oh, yes please!' they replied as one.

Pumpkin chose salted caramel and chocolate, Sweet P vanilla and hazelnut. It was yummy, scrummy, and delicious as only Italian ice cream can be.

Pumpkin seemed distracted. 'Why do you look so thoughtful, Pumpkin?'

'It's that table over there, the one on its side, not being used. Don't you think it would be really useful? It wouldn't take much to fix the broken leg.'

'Useful for sure, but where on earth could we stash it? It's such a funny shape to pack.'

'We could take the legs off and strap it to the bike rack, of course.'

'Of course,' groaned Sweet P, as Pumpkin sidled over to the friendly waitress who had been so nice to them.

She sighed as Pumpkin returned carrying the small round table awkwardly. She looked rather pleased with herself.

Back at *Van Rouge*, Pumpkin quickly found the screwdrivers, removed the legs, and packed them down the side of the bed.

'Hmm, how do we tie this to the bike rack?' asked Pumpkin, holding the table top tight to her chest. 'If only we could store it under the bed.'

'Ah yes, but given it's already stuffed with bricks, that is not going to happen,' said Sweet P.

Pumpkin decided to ignore this. A few minutes later, she had drilled two holes through the tabletop, so she could tie it onto the bike rack.

'We're starting to look like scrap merchants!' said Sweet P, resigned once again to the additional 'luggage'. 'I'll drive!'

Neither felt like driving very far after all the fun and games that day. They quickly found a lovely spot off road, near the lake. It was the perfect location. They could swim and then wash their dirty clothes using the water from the lake.

They cooked a tasty meal of spaghetti in tomato sauce with Italian cheese and some green leaves (they obviously had to keep themselves healthy).

Night arrived, the stars came out and moonlight glistened on the lake. Sweet P played a lullaby on her fiddle under the big full moon.

And then it was time for bed.

# – CHAPTER NINE –
## AUTOSTRADA MADNESS
## AND PIZZA

**Italian Words:**
*È molto bello = e m-O-l-t-oa (rhymes with 'go') b-E-l-oa*
= it's very beautiful
*Si = s-ee (rhymes with 'pea') = yes*
*Autostrada = ow-t-oa-s-t-r-ar-d-a* = motorway
*Perfetto = p-e-r-f-e-t-oa = perfect*
*Galles = G-A-l-ai-s* = Wales
*Siesta = s-ee-E-s-t-a* = afternoon rest or nap during
the hottest hours of the day in a hot climate
*Plaza = p-l-AR-z-a* = square *(not the maths sort!)*

**Welsh Word:**
*Bara Brith = b-a-r-a b-r-ee-th* = a traditional, Welsh
tea bread, usually made with raisins, currants and
candied peel

Sweet P opened her eyes and jumped out of bed.
She quickly put on her swimming costume and
went outside to the lake. With a yelp, she plunged
into the water. The duck family swam silently past

without even a nod of recognition in her direction.

As they did so Sweet P noticed a rather elegant couple – a shiny zucchini with a small clipped beard, and long thin pepper, wearing bright red pointy stilettos and an enormous pink straw hat – set up their picnic furniture by the water's edge. She watched the couple take out their books, a flask of coffee and two cups, and then settle down to read.

Pumpkin rolled out of bed. She needed a cup of tea before she could even think of swimming or eating. As she was making it she spotted the zucchini and pepper. She wandered over, cup of tea in hand, to greet them.

'Ah, *buongiorno!*' she said.

'*Buongiorno, signorina,*' said the zucchini.

'*È molto bello!*' said the zucchini.

'*Si!*' said Pumpkin.

Sweet P joined Pumpkin to find her standing in a funny position, with one leg sticking out and both arms stretched in front of her in a 'V' shape.

'*È* England,' said Pumpkin, shaking her leg. '*È* Scotland,' shaking her head. '*È* Wales,' she said, while wiggling her outstretched arms. 'This is where we come from, Wales,' she said, still wiggling her arms.

'*Si si, Galles!*' bellowed the dapper zucchini while the pepper looked away (she was not sure what to make of all this, nonsense probably).

After her swim Sweet P was starving. It was time for breakfast, muesli for Sweet P and eggs for Pumpkin. A burnt smell wafted through the air.

'Sheesh peesh, I never seem to get my toast quite right!' moaned Pumpkin. Toast rarely worked for her, anywhere. It always seemed to burn.

Once they had finished breakfast, they packed up and set off, Pumpkin at the wheel. It was a hot day already.

'OK, on the next part of our journey we use the *autostrada*. It will take us all the way to the ferry at Ancona,' said Sweet P, peering at the upside down road map.

'Have you got the tickets for the ferry, Sweet P?'

'Er, um, yes, but let me see, where are they?' She rustled around in the glove box. For a short while she could not find them and Sweet P looked worried.

'Phew, got them! Ferry goes tomorrow at 5.30pm – plenty of time.'

She breathed a sigh of relief.

Twenty minutes later, they drove onto the *autostrada*. It was very busy, with cars travelling at great speed.

'Get off my tail!' cried Pumpkin, as the car behind

edged extremely close to *Van Rouge*.

When the car overtook them, Sweet P leaned out of the window and squeezed Pig many times. '*Oink, oink, oink... squeak, squeak, squeak.*'

'Oh dear, I think the heat is getting to Pig. He's losing his voice!'

It was very hot for Pig by the small sky windscreen, and for the red poppies, which were now wilted and forlorn. Sweet P put Pig on her lap to cool down. He had to be ready to 'oink' into action should any badly behaved driver cause a problem. He did finally find his voice, a very satisfying 'grunt' when a lorry whizzed by far too close to *Van Rouge*.

'Everyone is in a hurry!' said Sweet P.

'Everyone can go faster than us, that's for sure!' said Pumpkin, peeling herself off the seat. She had started to stick to it. 'And it's so hot!'

'It might help if we could turn the heater down!' said Sweet P, trying to turn the broken knob with a pair of tiny pliers. 'Not sure it's made a difference though!'

It hadn't.

Later that day, after they had each taken a turn driving, they pulled over. They were cheesed off with the crazy traffic. Pig had never worked so hard.

'Let's go to Modena for pizza,' suggested Pumpkin. 'It's only a little way off the road.'

'Yes, stop and pizza *è perfetto*, Pumps!'

In Modena they found a quiet shady *plaza* where they could park. Pumpkin immediately spotted an old, three-legged wooden stool that had been dumped in a public litterbin.

'We'll have that! It just needs a lick of paint,' she said, tying it onto the bike rack underneath the table top with another bit of old rope. 'Now for a cup of tea.'

Sweet P looked through the cupboards and pulled out two packets of Welsh cakes and a *bara brith*.

'We can eat one of these packets. I have a cunning plan for the rest. You'll see!' She popped the second packet and the *bara brith* into her rucksack.

They walked through the streets and came across another beautiful *plaza* and found many more cafés. They soon spotted the sign they were looking for.

'Pizza!' Pumpkin cried.

'Wait here, Pumpkin,' said Sweet P, who set off to talk to the waiter, a pointy pepper with a neat black beard. He had a white serviette folded over his arm.

*What is she doing?* thought Pumpkin. From where she sat, she could see animated, smiling Sweet P holding out the Welsh cakes and *bara brith* to the confused pepper. He smiled and called out to a large tomato, who swaggered over. The large tomato was so red in the face he looked like he might burst out of his skin. *Ah, he must be the manager.*

'Over here, Pumpkin!' called Sweet P, sitting down at a small outside table under a yellow-and-green striped parasol. The waiter was laying out a paper tablecloth and clipping it around the sides, so it wouldn't blow away.

'I told you I had a clever plan! I swapped the *bara brith* and the Welsh cakes for two small pizzas! Handy that we just found out that *Galles* is the Italian word for Wales. Oh, and if we want *gelato* we can pop back this evening to do a spot of fiddling and juggling!'

'Well done, Sweet P!'

They high fived and then ordered from the large choice of pizzas: Margherita for Sweet P, Neapolitana for Pumpkin. Before long the pizzas arrived, served on wooden platters.

'Call these small, they are huge!' exclaimed Sweet P.

They were delicious too, like only Italian pizzas can be.

'I love Italian food,' she said with a sigh.

'I think I might need a *siesta* before we perform tonight,' said Pumpkin, burping.

So that's what they did. Back at *Van Rouge*, they set out their chairs under a tree and snoozed.

It was very late that night when they returned from their performance: happy, full of *gelato* and exhausted.

# – CHAPTER TEN –
## LOST AT SEA

***Italian Words:***
*Per favore* = *p-e-r f-a-v-OR-ai* = please
*Chi e* = *k-EE-e* = who is it?
*Benvenuto* = *b-e-n-v-e-n-OO-t-oa* = welcome

The sun had been up a while and it was hot in *Van Rouge*. Sweet P awoke with a start and looked at the clock by the bed.

'Pumpkin, it's gone half past ten and we still have a long way to go.'

'Yeah, it's late! I juggled for so long last night that I've been juggling all night in my dreams!' said Pumpkin.

'I think I played every tune I know!'

They had a quick cuddle, then shot out of bed and opened the curtains to find Modena awake, and on the move.

'I'm quite hungry though, I need some muesli or I'll fall into a heap!' said Sweet P.

'And I need my cup of tea or I'll dry into a pile of dust!'

'OK, ten minutes and counting. Go!' cried Sweet P, already filling her bowl.

Eighteen and a half minutes later, they were driving out of the *plaza*, following signs back to the *autostrada*.

'Ancona here we come! Wow, what a lot of traffic,' said Sweet P.

'You've got to be kidding me!' groaned Pumpkin as they quickly came to a standstill. There were cars and lorries barely moving for as far as they could see.

'Look at those beautiful yellow flowers.' Pumpkin jumped out of *Van Rouge* and picked a rather large bunch. She also found a charming but dirty sign that was lying near the flowers in the grass. It had a picture of a door knocker on it, with the word *'Benvenuto'* painted in red.

'We'll have that,' said Pumpkin.

She brushed the sign and squeezed it under the bed, while Sweet P emptied the tin of poppies and filled it with water. She then popped the flowers in, and placed them by the windscreen. They looked lovely.

'Let's have another cup of tea while we wait,' said Pumpkin.

'Not for me, thanks,' said Sweet P. 'Too much tea will make me wee!'

Tea (for Pumpkin) and several biscuits later, followed by I Spy and map reading, and they still had not moved more than a hundred metres. They had been on the road for two and a half hours in sweltering heat. Getting to the ferry on time was now looking doubtful.

'I think I'll melt if we don't move soon!' said Sweet P.

'Looks like we're going to miss the ferry,' said Pumpkin.

'Hey, I spy with my little eye something beginning with C,' said Sweet P.

'Er, cars, but look, they are actually starting to move. Finally!' yelled Pumpkin at the same time as Sweet P clambered back into the driver's seat.

'*Caramba*, let's go! Move these flowers over, Pumps, I can barely see out! It's two and a half hour's driving, and if we add half an hour for *Van Rouge* time, it will be five when we get there, and the ferry leaves at half past five.

'Hoody doody. Yes, that is cutting it close,' said Pumpkin.


Nearly three hours later, they were zooming up the wrong road at the port of Ancona.

'Where are you going, Sweet P? The port is that way!'

'Oh no, sorry!' cried Sweet P, as she did a quick u-turn. 'Can you get the tickets ready?'

'We have to collect them at the kiosk before boarding! Sheesh peesh!' Pumpkin shook her head.

On arrival at the kiosk, Pumpkin raced over to the ticket desk while Sweet P kept the engine running. She jumped back in and they raced off to the ferry. *Would they make it?* In the distance a big lorry was driving on board. Then the port worker onions began to lift the ramp.

Up it went...

Was it too late?

'Stop, *per favore* stop!' yelled Sweet P to a startled-looking onion.

For a moment the onion turned away and shouted at a tall French leek (he was saying '*oh lá lá*'). The leek's arms were moving frantically and he looked extremely cross. Finally the large onion stomped over to them.

'Tickets!' he said.

Pumpkin produced the tickets. Sweet P smiled broadly, the onion just grunted. He put a sign on their windscreen under the wiper blades. 'Go!' he said.

The other onions lowered the ramp and *Van Rouge* clanked noisily onto it and up to a very full garage deck. A tomato – with tatooed arms and looking hot like only a tomato can – was directing them into a tiny space.

They were on their way.

The sign on the windscreen said 'PATRAS'. This was their destination in Greece, twenty-three hours later. They took the steps from the garage deck into the main body of the ferry and paused to look at a ferry plan. It showed them what and where everything could be found on each of the four decks: the cabins, cafeterias, lounges, bars, restaurants, shop, children's area and the open deck itself.

There was so much to explore, but first they had to show their tickets at reception. A friendly artichoke greeted them. She had silvery hair and was wearing red lipstick and a smart blue uniform.

'It is no longer possible to sleep in campervans on board, but we are pleased to offer you a cabin *signorine.*'

'Wow, how fantastic is that!' said Sweet P. Admittedly she had rather looked forward to sleeping in *Van Rouge* on the ferry.

A steward, an older chestnut with a tan, led them down passage after passage. He stopped at number 916.

'Please, *signorine*, your cabin.'

It was small but cosy with bunk beds either side, and a tiny bathroom. Best of all was the window. Pumpkin took the top bunk and Sweet P took the bottom one on the opposite side. Sweet P produced some bread, pizza, biscuits and two apples she had saved from the day before. They unpacked all the food and had a yummy picnic dinner looking out to sea. The ferry sailed out of Ancona on its way to mainland Greece. Pumpkin felt suddenly sleepy and lay down to snooze.

'I just need a few minutes' doze, Sweet P.'

'I'm going to explore! See you later then, Pumpkin.'

Sweet P closed the door softly behind her. She walked down the long corridor, excited to explore the ferry. There were folk of all ages and nationalities eating in the cafeterias, some drinking in the bars, some watching huge TV screens. They were talking in Italian, Greek and languages she had never heard before. There were some British parsnips looking rather burned, probably because they had had a bit too much sun. A pair of Swedes looked very sporty in their tracksuits and white trainers. Little beans and baby beets jumped up and down in the soft playroom while their mamas and papas looked in the shop for bargains. Many truck drivers huddled into the smoking lounge.

Sweet P climbed the wide stairs to another deck.

A family of five: Mama, Papa Bean and three baby beans were snuggling down under blankets.

From here, Sweet P found her way onto the open

deck. She was nearly blown off her feet as she opened the heavy door. They had left port and she had a different view from each side of the ferry. Lights were starting to twinkle on the Italian shore and night was drawing in. On the other side it was just sea and more sea. It was all so amazing, blowy, wild and exciting. She soon realised how tired she was.

*Where's my bed?* she thought, a slight feeling of panic stirring in her tummy. Sweet P found it very easy to get lost. *What's our cabin number? Ah the key, that will say.*

She had a lot of pockets to feel in. *No key! I didn't bring it with me! But I know it's 961!*

Finally finding the right end of the ship and the right deck for the cabins, she spotted 'Cabins 890-991'. She followed the sign down the corridor. It had been a very long walk when she knocked on door, 961.

'*Chi e?*' said a gruff voice. It was certainly not Pumpkin's orange-topped pumpkin voice. *Must be 861.*

791-890 on another floor, knock knock.

'Go away!' said sleepy voice. *Must be 869.* 'Do Not Disturb' sign, *wrong again*, panic setting in, running. *Think and keep calm! But I'm sure it was 9 something!*

She raced back up to the floor above. *What*

*number, 969? Crying children, not that cabin. Which cabin?* How would she find it, help! A wrinkly turnip in the smart blue ferry uniform called to her: 'Are you lost, miss? Show me your key.'

'That's the problem, I left it in our cabin!'

'Please, miss, will you follow me.' Sweet P would have followed him to the moon if it meant finding her bed for the night. He took her to the reception desk, where she explained her sorry situation.

'Your name please?'

Within seconds she had her number: 916.

'Ah,' said Sweet P, 'but I'm sure that's where I went!'

No one believed her of course.

'Please to follow me, miss,' and off went the wrinkly turnip without waiting a second longer. Sweet P knocked at 916, and after what seemed an age, a bleary-eyed Pumpkin opened the door, muttering, 'Why didn't you take your key? You've woken me up, Sweet P!' and climbed back into bed.

Feeling lonely in her single bunk bed, Sweet P curled up and was soon running down long passages in her dreams.

Pumpkin awoke in the middle of the night and crept out to explore on her own. She didn't forget her key, but she did forget the time. It was very late when she quietly climbed back into her bunk.

# – CHAPTER ELEVEN –
## THE 'HEN' SITUATION

*Greek Words* (not in Greek letters!):
*Aftó eínai Igoumenítsa = a-f-t-OA*
*EE-n-e I-g-oo-m-e-n-EE-t-s-a* = That is Igoumenítsa
*Apó pou eísai? = a-p-OA*
*P-oo EE-s-e* = Where are you from?
*Oualía = W-a-l-EE-a* = Wales
*Eíste apó tin Oualía = EE-s-t-e a-p-OA t-ee-n W-a-l-*
*EE-a* = You are from Wales
*Korítsia = k-o-r-I-t-s-ee-a* = girls
*Polý kalá = po-l-EE k-a-l-A* = very well/good
*Tin echo = t-ee-n E-ch-oa* = I have it
*Ya sena = y-a s-e-n-a* = for you
*Ochi = O-<u>ch</u>-ee (with a frog in your throat, like the*
*Scottish word 'lo<u>ch</u>') = no*
*Kóta sas = k-OA-t-a s-a-s* = your hen
*Antio = a-<u>th</u>-EE-oa* = goodbye

It was so dark in the cabin, with the blinds down,
that Sweet P and Pumpkin slept deeply. All of a
sudden, a long string of Greek words came out of
the ferry loudspeaker system, followed fortunately

by a long string of English words.

'Attention, ladies and gentlemen. Will all car and lorry passengers for Igoumenítsa proceed directly to the garages and prepare for disembarkation. Thank you.'

'Wake up, Pumpkin, we've arrived. We're in Greece!'

Pumpkin rolled over.

Sweet P leapt out of her bunk. 'Wake up, Pumps, wake up!'

'What? But I haven't finished sleeping!'

'But we've gotta go! We're just coming into port!'

'Hang on. We don't arrive in Patras until four this afternoon. It can't be that time already,' said Pumpkin sleepily.

'Ah. Oh, sorry, Pumps! Yes, she did say Igou somewhere, and it's only quarter to ten. Phew! But we might as well go on deck and have our first look at Greece?'

'Give me a minute to wake up, Sweet P!'

One minute (and a bit) later, they were loading a rucksack. They popped in all the important things they needed: cabin keys, biscuits, tea bags, two juicy Sicilian oranges, sun cream, sunglasses, the *Teach Yourself Greek* book, maps of Greece, and a book each.

A few minutes later, they climbed the stairs to the open deck. The ferry was coming into a small port.

'Excuse me, where are we, please?' Sweet P asked a posh Greek radish with long red hair. The radish was leaning against the deck railing. Sweet P felt embarrassed to have to use English and promised herself to read the *Teach Yourself Greek* book later that day.

'*Aftó eínai Igoumenítsa,*' said the radish.

'Sorry, Igou where?' Sweet P couldn't help but notice her twinkly, high-heeled sandals.

'*I-g-oo-m-e-n-EE-t-s-a,*' replied the helpful radish. '*Apó pou eísai?*'

'Um? *Apo...?*'

'Where are you from?' asked the radish.

Pumpkin pretended to be a map again. Sweet P mimed driving.

'*Eíste apó tin Oualía!*' said the twinkly radish, laughing delicately. 'Ah! You drive from Wales to Greece?'

*She speaks good English. And she knows where Wales is,* thought Sweet P, who was very impressed.

'Yes, from *Oualía!*' said Sweet P, pleased to use a Greek word.

'Bravo, *korítsia! Polý kalá!*' cried the radish, smiling broadly. Pumpkin and Sweet P felt very proud and Sweet P beamed her wide smile.

As they arrived at the port of Igoumenítsa, overlooked by some very high mountains, the ramp began to drop. Vehicles and foot passengers queued on the dockside ready to board the ferry.

'We've made it to Greece, hoooweeee!' whooped Sweet P, looking ecstatic. Pumpkin looked embarrassed and pretended not to be with Sweet P.

They watched a portly aubergine wobbling towards the ramp on an old bicycle; his basket was full of brown paper parcels, all different sizes. A port pepper waved at him to stop.

The little port was very busy: cars were honking and huge lorries were driving in. In no time at all, the vehicles and foot passengers disembarked from the ferry. Soon after, the vehicles on land were given permission to board. A group of folk clutching their bags and cases were walking up the ramp.

'Breakfast!' said Sweet P. 'I'm so hungry!'

Sweet P and Pumpkin made their way to the ferry café. They asked for free cups of hot water, into which they popped their tea bags. They had their breakfast on deck, and each taking turn to look through the binoculars, they watched the port recede into the distance.

After a while, a British pot-bellied parsnip, wearing a baseball cap, and a turnip and two leeks, wearing vests, shorts, socks and sandals, plumped themselves down next to Sweet P and Pumpkin. Sweet P edged away as they spread their limbs out in the sun. Pumpkin watched as they each removed a bottle of beer from a cool box, and munched on pizza slices.

'This is the life, eh?' said the parsnip to no one in particular.

'So, where do you girls come from?' asked his friend, a red-faced tatooed turnip.

'We drove from Wales,' said Sweet P.

'*Duw duw,* I live in South Wales, in the valleys, I do,' said a black-haired, lean leek.

'Yer what, you girls drove from Wales, leave the guys behind did you, ha ha?' interrupted the pot-bellied parsnip, his belly shaking with laughter.

'Yep, the two of us are driving,' replied Sweet P coolly.

'I thought I saw you getting out of an old van, a red one with junk on the back. 'That yours, is it?' asked the tatooed turnip.

'That's right... and it's not junk. We're recycling,' said Pumpkin.

'Bit of an old crock, eh? How can you two drive that anyway?' He and his friends had a long chuckle.

'Well,' said Pumpkin, 'we turn the key, put her into gear, and off we drive. Easy.'

Pumpkin and Sweet P buried themselves in their

map to make a point of not wanting to talk any more. This did not appear to work, so instead they wandered over to the railing and looked out over the side. The island of Corfu was coming into view. Swiftly they found another spot to sit, leaning against the funnel in its shade.

Within seconds, they had started to test each other on Greek words, but within minutes they had fallen asleep.

'Attention ladies and gentlemen. Will all car and lorry passengers for Patras proceed directly to the garages and prepare for disembarkation. Thank you.'

Awoken with a start, they thought they had plenty of time, so took a last look over the side of the ferry. The port of Patras was fast approaching.

They wandered down to their cabin and packed their bits and pieces and the remains of the previous night's picnic. Sweet P stuffed a last piece of bread into her mouth. It was a little stale. Pumpkin checked her red dot.

'What garage deck are we on, Pumpkin?'

'No idea, Sweet P, which one do you think we're on?'

With the deck deserted, they realised that time was of the essence, but which garage deck and which door?

They opened the first door and were met by rows of lorries starting their engines. They opened the next and saw hundreds of cars that were now revving their engines, ready to go. They could not see *Van Rouge* or any other campervans.

'I can't remember where we parked *Van Rouge*,' said Sweet P, not wanting to be lost again.

'Think!' said Pumpkin, getting ratty.

'What makes you think I'm not?' retorted Sweet P, a little hurt.

Vehicles had started to drive off the ferry; it was noisy, it was hot, it was very confusing. As they entered the garage on the deck below they were confronted by a lot of horns beeping.

'Follow those horns, Sweet P, I think they're hooting at us!'

'But how do they know where we are?'

'I mean they're hooting at *Van Rouge*. She's probably blocking the way!'

They followed the blaring horns. *Van Rouge* was indeed in the way. She had been last on the ferry and, in consequence, had to leave first. They sheepishly climbed in, ignoring the angry stares of other drivers and port workers' shaking fists.

With a bump, they drove down the ramp and out into the dazzling Greek sunshine. It was exciting, but which way to Piraeus?

They stopped inside the port

to try to work it out. A runner bean jogged past wearing tight shorts and earphones. *Would he know the way?* Before they had a chance to ask him, he had disappeared into the distance.

A tatty-looking van took off with its tailgate down, and a basket fell out. Pumpkin and Sweet P jumped quickly out of *Van Rouge*, calling, 'Hey, stop, come back, stop!'

They chased after the van shouting and waving, but to no avail. They returned to the basket to investigate. It looked well-used and it was quite big with a leather strap.

'Is there anything inside?' mused Pumpkin. 'Help, aagh, ow!' she cried as she opened the lid. An angry hen flew out and pecked her nose, right on her red dot.

Sweet P tried not to laugh, but failed badly. 'There's a hen to lay eggs for you, Pumps, but I bet you don't want to take her with us!'

The hen was running off and they didn't know what to do. *How do you catch an angry hen? And what would we do with an angry hen anyway?* thought Pumpkin, whose nose was now bright red.

'We can't just leave her. She's frightened,' said Sweet P.

The hen was causing a stir, and a fisher onion, with a grizzled beard, waved his arms at them. He looked angry as if they had done something wrong, but as he shouted to them they couldn't understand a word he was saying. They started to run after the hen and saw that a large olive on a bicycle was already chasing her, an old cloth sack in his hand. A uniformed port pepper joined the chase. Folk leaned out of their vehicles and laughed.

The olive flung the old sack over the hen. Instantly it became still. He then expertly manoeuvred the hen into the sack.

'*Korítsia! Tin écho!*'

Sweet P and Pumpkin joined the commotion. The fisher onion and port pepper did not look pleased.

'*Ya sena korítsia!*' said the olive.

They weren't sure what he was saying, but they certainly didn't want what he was holding out to them,

'*Ochi, efcharistó*, Mr Olive!' Pumpkin shook her head.

'*Ya sena!*' said Sweet P, smiling at him and pointing from the sack to the olive. The olive shook his head and put the sack containing the hen on the ground.

'*Ochi korítsia, kóta sas!*' he said, pointing his gnarly finger at them. He turned and pedalled off waving.

'*Antio!*'

The pepper and the fisher onion tut tutted, shook their heads and went back to their business.

'Oh no, now what? We can't leave the hen like this,' said an exasperated Pumpkin, rubbing her sore red nose.

'Yes, we are in a pickle. Have you seen your nose, Pumps? Let me get you some cream.'

The cream did help, but it didn't help the 'Hen Situation'.

'Sheesh peesh!' moaned Pumpkin.

'Hoody flipping poody,' said Sweet P with a sigh.

*

Back at Van Rouge they carefully emptied Hen into the basket and shut the lid quickly.

'Well, at least she can breathe in there, and she's had a run. But what should we do with her, Pumps?'

'I don't know. And what do hens eat?' asked Pumpkin, crumbling some biscuits and throwing them quickly into the basket. She shut the lid swiftly before Hen could nip her again.

Finally, they had found something Pumpkin did not want. And there was nowhere to put Hen or her basket other than on Pumpkin's lap. Sweet P climbed into the driver's seat. They still did not know which way they were going.

# – CHAPTER TWELVE –
## KOSTA'S DISHES

*Greek Words:*
*Sygnómi* = *s-i-g-n-OA-m-ee* = excuse me/sorry
*Pou?* = *p-oo?* = where?
*Lesvos* = *L-e-s-v-o-s* = the island of Lesvos
*Ne* = *n-e* = yes
*Geia sas!* = *y-A s-a-s!* = hello!
*Tavérna* = *t-a-v-AIR-n-a* = tavern, café
*Dolmádes* = *th-o-l-m-AR-d-e s* = stuffed vine leaves
*Rígani* = *r-I-g-a-n-ee* = oregano
*Tsip* = *t-s-i-p* = chips
*Eínai polý zestó* = *EE-n-e p-o-l-EE z-e-s-t-OA*
*Efcharistó polý* = *e-f-ch-a-r-i-s-t-OA p-o-l-EE* = thank
you very much
*Sas efcharistoúme* = *s-a-s e-f-ch-a-r-i-s-t-OO-m-ai* = we
thank you
*Kalinychta* = *k-a-l-EE-n-i-c-t-a* = Goodnight


*\* Ornamental Gourd: the dried, hard and hollowed-out
shell of any plant belonging to the gourd family. It's often
used as a container or ornament*

Sweet P and Pumpkin followed the traffic hoping to see signs to Piraeus. It was a big port after all, so surely it would be signposted.

There was such a lot of traffic, one-way systems, and name places in Greek with letters they could not even recognise. It was all a bit overwhelming. Sweet P managed to pull off the busy road and switch the engine off.

'Phew! Right, where are we going?'

They pored over the map. Piraeus is the port of Athens, which is the capital of Greece. They could see Piraeus on the map, but they needed to find a road sign that matched. Sweet P grabbed the *How To Speak Greek* book. She found *sygnómi* for 'excuse me,' pronounced *s-i-g-n-OA-m-ee*, and *pou* for 'where', pronounced *p-oo*. That was a good start. She called to a passing broad bean, wearing a pink sunhat and large sunglasses, '*Sygnómi! Pou* Piraeus?' *Fancy saying poo as a proper word,* she thought with a chuckle.

All they understood from the stream of strange words was '*Peiraiás*', which sounded a bit like 'Piraeus', and that an arm was pointing in the opposite direction to the one they were facing.

'Thank you, *gracias, merci,* thank you in Greek!' she called.

They turned round with difficulty and entered the stream of traffic.

'Sheesh peesh, these signs look like gobbledy gook! How are we supposed to know which one to follow?' asked Pumpkin.

'It's all Greek to me!' said Sweet P, pleased with her joke.

'Look a sign to *Athína*. That must be Athens, turn here!' cried Pumpkin, back on the case. 'And now one to *Peiraiás!* That's a relief, it looks like each sign is repeated in English* letters a bit further on!'

Αθήνα = *Athína* = A-th-EE-n-a = Athens
Πειραιάς = *Peiraiás* = P-ee-r-ai-A-s = Piraeus
*Actually Roman letters

They joined the road to Athens and Piraeus, a very busy thoroughfare to the coast. Soon they could see a huge white suspension bridge glistening in the sunshine. It spanned the Gulf of Korinth.

'Pumpkin, should we take the old road?' said Sweet P looking at the map. 'It runs through the seaside towns. We could maybe find a nice beach to swim and chill. What do you reckon?'

'*Ne!*' said Pumpkin.

'Why not? I don't understand?'

'*Ne*, I said *ne!*'

'Why not say yeah, instead of *ne*, or do you really not like that idea?' Sweet P was exasperated.

'*Ne* is Greek for yes!'

'Oh, I see, well it sounds like "no"!'

'Poo!' said Sweet P, a moment later.

'*Pou?* Where? Where what?'

'Can't you smell Hen? She's done a poo!'

'Yuck, it's seeping out of the basket. Disgusting!' said Pumpkin.

With the smell being so bad, they quickly found a lovely quiet spot on a narrow, sandy beach. They parked *Van Rouge* in the shade of some tamarisk trees. It was half past five. Behind them were mountains, with the sea in front. It really did all feel *very* Greek.

Oh, and they'd forgotten about the 'Hen situation'.

They quickly looked in *Van Rouge* for something for Hen to eat. 'We can give her a bowl of water in the shade and some breadcrumbs. And if she decides to leave, she can do just that!' said Pumpkin, still sore from her nipped nose and still rather put out.

They cleaned out Hen's basket, holding their noses, and put the old sack in the bottom. Pumpkin looked in the mirror and was horrified to see how enlarged and red her nose now appeared. And she smelt of hen poo.

She changed her shorts. Sweet P found a little bowl and filled it with water. Pumpkin scattered some food scraps.

'I was going to eat that cold piece of toast,

Pumps!'

'Too late now,' said Pumpkin as she ripped the toast into pieces and tossed it on the ground.

They gingerly opened the basket and jumped back. Hen hopped out with a squawk and strutted around looking rather indignant.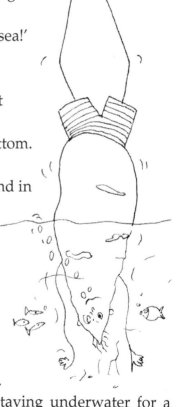

'Right, let's get in that sea!' said Pumpkin.

'You bet, race you!'

They ran across the hot sand and dived in.

'Wow, I can see the bottom. I can see my whole body.'

Sweet P did a handstand in the water, a wobbly one.

Pumpkin plunged in too. 'Bit warmer than the Irish Sea!'

There were no waves, but they played frisbee, diving underwater to rescue it each time it flew over their heads and sank.

Pumpkin seemed to be staying underwater for a long time. She came up, spluttering.

'Guess what I found down there?'

'The frisbee, I hope!'

'Yes, but I also found a fisherman's net half buried in the sand. I reckon it must have been there a long time and been forgotten about. Give me a hand. Grab this end, Sweet P.'

They pulled vigorously, but it would not shift. Sweet P dived down and scrabbled in the sand, while Pumpkin yanked until it finally wrenched free. It was green, not very big, and a bit slimy, but it was hole free.

'We'll have this! We can string it up and use it as a hammock! Good find, eh?'

'*Ne,*' said Sweet P, pleased to be using her new Greek word, 'and it will barely take up any space! Now this I like. It's small!'

Pumpkin hung it out to dry in the sun. They could not see Hen anywhere. But in the bottom of the basket was a warm...

'Egg!' cried Pumpkin. 'She's laid an egg!'

'She must have liked the sack in the bottom. Made it cosier, I suppose,' said Sweet P.

They looked at the egg in awe.

'Can we take it, Pumps?'

'We certainly can. That's payment for my sore nose!'

After looking around for Hen without success, they lay down to dry themselves in the sun. They studied their *How to Speak Greek* book and tested each other. It was tricky but fun.

'Cluck, cluck, cluck.' The hen strutted back, her baggy neck darting forward as she did so, and then she calmly hopped into her basket. Sweet P played her fiddle under the tree while Pumpkin juggled in time to the tune. Hen seemed quite calm and was making contented murmuring sounds.

'*Geia sas! Polý kalá!*' said an excited voice.

They stopped in surprise and saw a smiling aubergine with a large nose, standing there in pointy shoes. He appeared to be talking to them.

Seeing their blank looks, he spoke in English. 'Please, you will come to my *tavérna* to play? It is there, look. I give you good food, *ne*?' He was pointing at a small café, a *tavérna* just in from the beach, under a huge tamarisk tree, some hundred metres away. There were blue and white checked tablecloths on all the tables. All sorts of differently shaped gourds* hung under the shady pergola, blowing gently in the breeze. They were painted different colours: some spotty, some striped, some bright colours. It all looked very enticing.

Pumpkin and Sweet P exchanged a look. 'Let's go!' they replied. Pumpkin, however, was embarrassed about her large red nose. Before setting off, she touched it up a little to make it look like it was supposed to be like that.

They played and juggled beautifully and the customers clapped heartily. Pumpkin even gave the customers a little shine with her sparkly feather duster. Then Sweet P and Pumpkin realised just how hungry they were.

'Sit, my friends, I bring you Kosta's best dishes, you will see!' Out came a plate of *dolmades*, a plate of fried courgette flowers and another of homemade chips.

Pumpkin asked the waiter, a rather plump red onion with dangly earings, 'What's this on the chips?'

'Ah, in Greece we like to shake this *rígani* on our *tsip*. It is very nice, I think.'

Pumpkin looked in their *How to Speak Greek* book. 'Ah, that's oregano! No vinegar on your chips here, then?'

'Mmm, tasty, I like *rígani* on *tsip*!' said Sweet P,

eating a large forkful.

Finally, Kostas came to their table carrying a frying pan in which there was a piece of yellow cheese in flames. 'This is *Saganáki*, very good, you will like it. But it is hot, *ne*! *Eínai polý zestó.*'

And did they like it. It was mouth-wateringly delicious. They washed it all down with freshly squeezed lemonade.

'*Efcharistó!*' said Pumpkin, who had remembered the Greek word for 'thank you'.

'*Polý!*' said Sweet P who had remembered the Greek word for 'very much'.

'*Sas efcharistoúme! Kalinychta!*' called Kostas.

It was late by the time they got back to *Van Rouge*. Pumpkin jumped straight into bed and Sweet P was quick to follow, but had to clean her teeth first. Before she climbed up, she popped the basket lid down on Hen, who was sleeping.

'Thanks for the egg!' she whispered. She looked out into the distance.

'Can you see the twinkling lights of those fishing boats out to sea, Pumpkin?'

Pumpkin was already asleep Sweet P cuddled up and soon followed her. They dreamed to the sound of the lapping water of the Ionian Sea just a few metres away.

# – CHAPTER THIRTEEN –
## THE CHASE

**Greek Words:**
*Kyríes kai kýrioi = k-ee-r-EE-ai-s k-ai k-EE-r-ee* =
Ladies and gentlemen
*Katapliktikó! = k-a-t-a-p-l-i-k-t-i-k-OA* = amazing!
*Mytilíni = M-i-t-i-l-EE-n-ee* = Mytiline, the capital of
Lesvos

**French Word:**
*Voilà! = v-w-A-l-a* = Here/that's it!

Sweet P and Pumpkin awoke early and could hardly believe that they were actually in Greece. Sweet P opened the screechy sliding door and jumped back into bed.

'I think we're going to need some more oil on that door again,' said Pumpkin, peaking through the window. Sweet P joined Pumpkin at the window and they both stared at the turquoise sea. Two wooden fishing boats were heading to shore. *They must have been out working all night,* thought Sweet P.

'Tea in bed?' asked Pumpkin.

'Now you're talking!' replied Sweet P.

Pumpkin let Hen out, gave her water, some bits of leftovers, and then made the tea.

And so began a lazy morning of eating, swimming and playing frisbee.

Pumpkin went for a wander along the beach and Sweet P buried herself in her *Teach Yourself Greek* book in between swims. She learned a long word, *katapliktikó!* and practised it over and over.

An hour or two later, she heard a swishy sound and looked up to see Pumpkin dragging a bright orange parasol back along the beach.

'Look at this, Sweet P. I found it in a crevice in the rocks. It's not broken.'

'Wow, that's great!'

Within minutes, they dug a deep hole with their hands. They pushed the parasol into it and filled the hole with sand. Stamping it down firmly with their feet, they put a pile of stones around the base, then opened the parasol gingerly. V*oilà!* They now had shade very close to the sea's edge, where they could catch a breath of fresh air.

'*Katapliktikó!*' said Sweet P, chuffed with her new

word.

'Katapult... what did you say?'

'*K-a-t-a-p-l-i-k-t-i-k-OA*. It means amazing. I've just learned it. Rolls off the tongue with a bit of practice!'

'Cluck, cluck, cluck.' Hen had come to join them. She scratched down and flopped onto the cool sand. She closed her eyes and rolled around, legs and wings akimbo, making strange sounds.

The rest of the day was relatively quiet until the wind started to pick up. First it was a gentle breeze then it became a little stronger, and finally rather gusty.

'Hey, quick, catch it!' yelled Pumpkin as the wind yanked the parasol out of the sand. It took off down the beach, with Pumpkin and Sweet P chasing after it barefoot. Hen joined the chase, squawking wildly.

'Ouch, ouch, my feet are burning, the sand is red hot!' cried Sweet P, as they raced along.

'Mine too.'

In the distance they could see a portly pepper hurling himself at the parasol. He grabbed it as it flew past.

'Wow, seriously impressive!' they agreed. With the chase now over, they walked along the edge of the water to cool their burning feet.

'*Ya sas, efcharistó*, Mr Pepper!' said Sweet P. He was wearing purple boxer trunks and huge blue

sunglasses, red baseball cap in hand. 'This is your parasol, *ne korítsia*? You are lucky I catch it!' He looked very pleased with himself.

' *Ne, efcharistó,*' said Sweet P.

'*Polý!*' said Pumpkin.

' You are coming from which country?'

'We drove from *Oualía*,' said Pumpkin. Once again she pretended to be the map of Britain, emphasising Wales.

'You come from *Oualía* in that old van I see, *óchi!*'

'*Ne*, we did!' said Sweet P with a smile.

'Where is your driver, I don't see him. He is mending the van?'

Sweet P stopped smiling. 'Huh, you are looking at the drivers!'

'And *Van Rouge* does not need mending!' said Pumpkin crossly.

Hen arrived in a flurry of feathers and squawked loudly. As she jumped up and down the pepper took one step back. 'You are all crazy!' said the pepper.

'*Efcharistó polý* for catching the parasol. Have a nice day,' said Pumpkin.

Hen gave a last indignant squawk, as Sweet P and Pumpkin turned away and paddled back along the sea's edge to their spot down the beach. The wind kept catching the parasol like a sail. Carrying it was very tricky, until one of them (which one I wonder?) had the bright idea to close it.

'Cheeky flipping pepper, huh!' said Sweet P.

'I'd say, I reckon this parasol has blown along the beach before and the owner didn't want to chase after it,' said Pumpkin, as she laid their lunch out on a blue and white checked tablecloth: bread, cheese, plum tomatoes and apricots. 'Our luck!'

'Shoo!' cried Pumpkin as Hen tried to peck at their food. Surprisingly, on hearing this, Hen hopped back in her basket.

After lunch, and tea and biscuits to wash it down, Pumpkin and Sweet P swam in the sea, followed by a relaxing walk.

'Let's look at this map. We can choose which Greek island to go to, Sweet P,' said Pumpkin with a yawn.

'Good idea, Pumpkin!'

They stared at the map and looked at the many islands you can reach from Piraeus by ferry.

'You know, Pumps, I like the look of that big island not very far from Turkey.'

'You mean the one that looks a bit like a horseshoe?'

'Yes, exactly! Horseshoes are supposed to be lucky, aren't they? It's bigger than a lot of the other islands. That means lots of coastline, which means lots of beaches.'

'And plenty of land for our tiny home. It's called Lesvos. Well, why not? Let's go there!'

'And its name is easy to pronounce,' said Sweet P.

They high fived. Both were eager to leave straight away, but then Sweet P yawned too. She was feeling exhausted.

'You know, Pumpkin, it's getting late. I'm feeling sleepy.'

'Me too. Early dinner, early night, early start in the morning?' suggested Pumpkin.

'Good plan. What shall we have for dinner? Something easy?'

Dinner was actually very easy: eggy bread, cucumber and fruit. After this, Sweet P played some new Greek tunes while Pumpkin did the washing up.

Thirty minutes later, they drifted happily to sleep.

# – CHAPTER FOURTEEN –
## A WINDY NIGHT ON BOARD

*Greek Word:*
*Kalispéra* = *k-a-l-ee-s-p-AI-r-a* = Good evening
*Tholmádes* = th-o-l-m-AR-d-ai-s = stuffed vine
leaves, a traditional Greek dish of food
*Chíos* = <u>Ch</u>-EE-o-s (*as in lo<u>ch</u>, frog in your throat*) =
*Chíos (name of a Greek island)*

The following day, Pumpkin awoke quite late. As
she crawled out of bed, Sweet P stirred as well.
So much for the early start, but what did it matter?

Hen was still asleep.

They had a 'wake up and wash' swim in the sea,
and what turned into a lazy breakfast of muesli for
Sweet P, egg and burnt toast for Pumpkin.

Hen woke up and started cackling in her basket.
She seemed quite excited and was probably hungry
by now. Pumpkin scattered some crumbs and tasty
morsels. Hen ate them and strutted around looking
for more yummy delights. Pumpkin and Sweet P
packed everything away. They tied the parasol up
with a bit of rope, and squeezed it in between the

two hanging washing line poles.

'Right, we're off, Hen, so hop into your basket, chook!' encouraged Pumpkin.

Hen, however, had a different plan, and with a cluck she took off.

'We'll see about that,' said Sweet P. 'Climb aboard, Pumpkin, and grab her basket. Let's give her a surprise.'

They set off in *Van Rouge*.

After a moment Hen started to chase after them, flapping and clucking, until she was quite pooped, then simply flopped down. She didn't object when they lifted her into her basket.

Throughout the final two hours' drive to Piraeus, Sweet P studied the map in her usual fashion.

'Look out for the bridge over the Gulf of Korinth, Pumps. It doesn't look very wide. We'll cross it in a flash.'

Sweet P was poring over the map, trying to work out how much further it was to the bridge.

'Here it is...' *Zoom!* 'And there it was!' cried Pumpkin.

Sweet P looked dismayed. 'I can't believe I missed the bridge after all that!'

Half an hour later, they arrived at a huge, bustling port. Piraeus was much bigger than Patras, with many ferries coming and going.

'Just look at that enormous cruise ship. It looks like a huge layered cake,' said Sweet P. They could see folk hanging out of their balconies. 'And look, that ferry is probably like ours, I wonder where it's going?' Folk were waving as the ship hooted and loosed its moorings. They waved back.

'I wonder if there are any stowaways hiding on board,' mused Pumpkin.

They found the ticket office for the Greek islands:

Crete, the Cyclades Islands, the Dodecanese Islands, the Saronic Islands, the Aegean Islands, of which Lesvos is one. The ferry to Lesvos was due to leave at 8.00pm, so they had a bit of time to wander the port, and then pack their overnight bag.

'OK, so what do we need tonight? Food, toothbrushes, sleeping bags...' said Pumpkin, reaching for the rucksack to put them in.

'...Two pairs of knickers, pillows. Shame we won't have a cabin on this ferry, eh? Still, I reckon it will be lovely sleeping on deck. We'll just find a cosy space to ourselves,' said Sweet P.

'And Hen?' asked Pumpkin.

'Of course and Hen!'

The overnight ferry crossing to Mytiline, the main port of Lesvos, would take eleven hours, and they would arrive at 7.00am. The queue to board the ferry was rather quick and, within minutes, they were driving up the ramp.

They grabbed the rucksack, put Hen in her

basket, and climbed up the steps to the main decks.

The ferry fava beans greeted them. '*Kalispéra korítsia*, welcome aboard!'

'*Efcharistó*,' said Pumpkin

'*Polý*,' said Sweet P.

It was a warm, balmy evening.

'Let's find a spot for our picnic and set out our sleeping bags,' said Sweet P. 'What about over there by the two life rafts?'

They both agreed it would be a good spot, tucked away from where most folk were walking.

They left Hen in her basket guarding their gear and wandered around the different decks. The engines were humming and the ramp had just been raised. As they leaned against the ferry railings, they watched some lean, tanned potatoes unhook the huge ropes from the capstans on the quay. The ferry was on its way, slowly moving away from the dock. It was getting dark and the lights of the tugboats and ferries shone over the water.

They went back to Hen and ate their bread, feta cheese, *tholmádes*, peaches and Welsh cakes (there were still some left). As they ate, the wind grew stronger. It was trying to snatch the bread from the picnic box. They threw some food into Hen's basket. They could not let her out here, she would be blown away, and goodness knows where she would end up.

'Mmm, delicious,' said Pumpkin. 'Shall we have a quick walk before we go to sleep?'

At the stern of the ferry they watched the sea churning as the ship ploughed through it. They went to the port side and saw land, little pinpricks of light shining through the darkness.

'I wonder which island that is,' said Pumpkin.

'It could still be the mainland,' said Sweet P.

The deck was empty and there was no one around to ask. There wasn't even a map to show which islands they might be passing. They went to the starboard side and saw land in the distance. After a wander around outside, and having cleaned their teeth inside, they went back to the life rafts to get ready for bed. It was still rather windy.

'Shall we put Hen under this life raft to keep her out of the wind and stop her being whooshed overboard?' asked Pumpkin.

'Good idea!'

'Night night, Hen,' they called to her. She cooed and murmured in response.

Pumpkin was trying to get into her sleeping bag, but the wind had other ideas. 'Sheesh peesh! This isn't going to be as easy as I thought.'

Sweet P looked at her own thin sleeping bag and at Pumpkin's thick downy one. *Oh dear*, she thought, as she tussled with her bag in the wind, getting herself into quite a knot. Finally she managed to slither in.

'Wow, it's blowing a gale!' she cried.

'What did you say?!' yelled Pumpkin.

'It's really windy and I'm very cold!' shouted Sweet P.

'It's very windy and I'm very warm!' yelled Pumpkin, just as a piece of rope danced by her on the wind, nearly whipping her head. With her long arm and quick reactions, she managed to grab the end of it.

'Wow!' said Sweet P, impressed.

'Good timing, we'll have this!' said Pumpkin as the rope and her head disappeared into her bag. 'Night night, Sweet P!' she added as she stuck her head out once more.

'Night night,' replied Sweet P feebly. She shivered inside her woefully thin sleeping bag, feeling a little miserable. She was fully dressed but still cold. *What had she been thinking when she said it would be cosy sleeping outside?*

There was so much wind because the ferry was

moving and it was no longer the balmy breeze they had felt when they were moored in port. They were out on the open sea. A couple of uncomfortable hours passed for Sweet P.

'Right, that's it, I'm so cold I'm going to find somewhere inside to sleep before I go numb!' she called to an unresponsive blob beside her.

She left the dark night to enter the brightly lit ferry, looking longingly at the signs to the cabins, and climbed the stairs. There were people asleep everywhere; in any space you could roll out a sleeping bag or blanket, every one was taken. Finally she decided on a spot in between two rows of empty air seats where only a low light shone. She curled up and pulled her sleeping bag over her head and tossed and turned until she finally dozed off.

Some little time later...

'*Kyríes kai kýrioi,*' boomed the loud speaker, and continued in a stream of Greek, awaking Sweet P with a jolt. She only understood the beginning, ladies and gentlemen and something about the garages and *Chíos*.

*It must be asking folk for Chíos to disembark,* thought Sweet P. She was awake now so decided to venture back on deck. She followed the snores to Pumpkin.

'Pumpkin, wake up, we're stopping at *Chíos*. Do you want to take a look?'

Groggy though she was, Pumpkin did not want

115

to miss out.

They could see the lights of the port, traffic lining up to get onto the ferry, the port peppers busy doing their jobs. The ferry was slowly turning and edging its stern into the dockside. Crew on board threw big fat ropes to the waiting hands of the onshore onions, who looped the ropes over huge capstans to secure the ferry. Then the ramp was noisily lowered and any cars disembarking were directed to drive off the ferry. Several foot passengers walked on with sacks and boxes, barrels full of olives, cheeses, pots and pans. Then followed cars, motorbikes, mopeds and a couple of lorries. There was quite a bustle for four in the morning. Car headlights lit up the mountains as they snaked along the roads behind the port.

Sweet P and Pumpkin wandered back to their sleeping bags.

'Why don't you cuddle up, Sweet P? That way you'll keep warm and we can be on deck together?'

Sweet P liked the sound of this and went to retrieve her sleeping bag.

Moments later, they snuggled into a deep sleep, but before they knew it, they were awoken again by...

'Kyríes kai kýrioi—' They were coming into Mytiline. Sweet P and Pumpkin lingered a while. It was nicer on deck than waiting in the garage in a huddle of folk.

'Oh, that's an impressive fortress up on the hill!' said Pumpkin.

'I love all those tavérnes and cafés by the waterside,' said Sweet P, 'and look at all those boats moored along the quay. I can't believe we've arrived! *Geia sas Lesvos!*'

# – CHAPTER FIFTEEN –
## A NEW FRIEND

*Arabic Word:*
*Marhaban! = M-ar-h-A-b-a-n* = Hello!

'M*arhaban!*' said a quiet disembodied voice from above.

'Did you hear that, Sweet P?'

'What?'

'A voice, coming from the life raft over there.'

Pumpkin pointed to the life raft at the top of the ladder.

'Hello, I am here,' said the voice once again. An aubergine wearing a red scarf around her head popped her head through the canvas door on the side of the life raft.

'Oh, goodness, are you a stowaway?' asked Sweet P in awe.

The colourful aubergine disappeared inside the raft again and spoke through the side.

'Please, don't give me away. Will you help me leave the ship?'

Pumpkin and Sweet P looked at each other in

disbelief – a stowaway. They wanted desperately to help her.

'No one is around now. Everyone's leaving the ferry. We'll help you as best we can,' said Pumpkin. 'Just climb down.'

Once the aubergine had descended the ladder, Pumpkin and Sweet P introduced themselves.

'And this is Hen, she's a stowaway too!' said Sweet P, opening the basket lid for Hen to give a quick hello.

'Cluck, cluck.'

'I am Amina,' said the young, thin and frightened

aubergine. 'I leave my home, my parents and little sister. It is bad in Syria; there is much fighting. My parents say you children are young. You must go and find a new life! With my brother, I crossed the sea from Turkey in a boat to this island. We were many people, and I thought we were drowning. We live in a very big camp with other refugees like us, from many countries. I did not like it, so I went on a ferry to Athens, but I was lonely and scared in the city; nowhere to stay, no money, no papers. Now I come back to Lesvos to be with my brother again. It is better. The camp is not a good place to live, but it is somewhere.'

She reached into her small bundle of possessions and brought out a ragged photo of her mama, papa, little sister and brother. She held it out to show her new friends.

'Your family look very nice,' said Pumpkin.

'Thank you! But what if they stop me leaving the ferry?'

'We will hide you in our van, Amina. You might be a bit squashed though,' said Sweet P.

'Squashed? What means squashed?' she asked.

'You'll soon understand! You speak good English.'

'I learn at school,' said Amina.

In the next few minutes they worked out a plan. Amina would follow them closely. She would walk among the other foot passengers, who would have to pass through the garages.

'Don't lose us,' whispered Sweet P.

Luckily there were a few aubergines, zucchinis and other folk queuing with their bundles and bags ready to leave the ferry. Amina quietly tucked herself in among them.

'OK, so which garage are we in, Sweet P?'

'The bottom garage,' said Sweet P, although she didn't look very certain.

'Huh! You don't know, do you? We're B Garage, down these steps,' said Pumpkin.

And she was exactly right. 'I'll go ahead to make space in *Van Rouge* for Amina.'

Pumpkin opened the sliding door with a screech, quietly groaning. *That flipping door!* she thought as she quickly moved all the bags and boxes into the cab and grabbed the blanket that would cover Amina. Sweet P arrived at *Van Rouge*, Amina a moment later.

'Quick, get in and climb up, Amina,' said Sweet P, pointing to the high bed. They hoped no one was watching.

As soon as Amina was inside and had climbed onto the bed, Sweet P pulled the screechy door shut. *Ooch!* From the cab Pumpkin threw the blanket over Amina, then leaned over to pile the bags and boxes on top of her. Two bags started to slip off. Sweet P opened the sliding door just in time, caught the bags and gently pressed down on Amina, whispering, 'Lie flat, Amina!' There was a muffled sigh from under the blanket as the lump went flatter. Sweet P rearranged the bags and boxes to cover her as completely as possible. Soon they were clanking down the ramp into the small port. It was early morning in Mytiline, beautifully warm, not yet the sizzling hot day it would be in a couple of hours.

'Stop!' called a customs onion, signalling where to pull over.

'Oh no, here we go. Be still and quiet, Amina!' said Sweet P as *Van Rouge* came to a halt.

'You will open your doors,' said the plump, officious onion.

Trying to look nonchalant, Sweet P opened them all while Pumpkin put out the two folding chairs. They would be comfortable while they waited.

Punpkin and Sweet P held their breaths.

The officious onion walked around Van Rouge,

inspecting the wheels and headlights.

Amina tried not to breathe as another customs officer, a thin bean, peered around inside, prodding bags and boxes.

*Please don't poke Amina,* thought Sweet P.

*Please stay quiet, Amina,* thought Pumpkin.

*Please don't prod me,* thought Amina, holding herself rigid.

*What's going on now?* thought Hen, resisting a cluck.

The customs onion and his thin bean sidekick were baffled and irritated to see the high-rise bed and the pallets stacked underneath the mattress. There were bricks under the bed itself, bags and boxes on top of it and two poles and a parasol strung up in the roof. Bits of broken furniture hung from the bike rack. They gave each other bemused looks. The skinny bean shrugged.

'Cup of tea?' called Pumpkin to the exasperated officers, trying to distract them.

'*Ochi, efcharistó,*' snapped the plump onion. He moved to the cab, opened the basket and Hen flew up into his face. He snapped it shut quickly. Pumpkin and Sweet P tried not to laugh.

Red with indignation, 'You can go!' he said irritably.

'Sheesh peesh, and thank goodness for that,' said Pumpkin under her breath. She got back into *Van*

*Rouge,* put on her seatbelt and waited for Sweet P to join her. She then drove away slowly, resisting speeding away from the customs folk in case they changed their minds.

Poor Amina was making very uncomfortable sounds and whimpers as they drove along the road by the sea. They needed to find a private breakfast and 'what to do next' stop.

Just a little way along the coast road they pulled onto a wide piece of rough ground. Here there were two large containers parked up, ready to be connected to lorry cabs at some point. Pumpkin had stopped on the sea-facing side of one of them to give them some privacy from the road.

'You can get out now, Amina!' said Sweet P, opening the side door. She pulled everything off her as fast as she could. Amina emerged panting, looking very hot and very squashed.

'Thank you so much, yes, squashed!' she said, gasping for air.

*She certainly knows the meaning of that word now,* thought Sweet P as she offered her chair to Amina to sit on. Pumpkin made them all a nice pot of tea.

'You can get out now, Hen,' said Sweet P, opening the basket. Hen hopped out, pleased to stretch her legs.

'Wow, another egg!' Pumpkin carefully picked it up. 'Breakfast! Amina, do you like egg?'

'Thank you, I like egg,' replied Amina.

'We now have two, so I'll make an omelette for us all to share.'

Sweet P poured the tea and found some bread and cheese to go with it, followed by fruit for afters. She gave the last Welsh cake to Amina. They ate their breakfast by the water's edge, watching all the early morning activity in the distance.

'We can take you to the camp if you can show us the way,' said Sweet P sadly, 'I'm really not sure what else we can do.'

'There's not enough room for three of us to sleep in *Van Rouge*,' said Pumpkin, shaking her tufty head.

Just then another aubergine popped out from behind the other container. She looked a little like Amina and had a multi-coloured scarf wrapped around her head.

Amina's eyes lit up. 'She is my friend!' she cried.

The aubergine spotted Amina and ran towards her. Soon the two of them were hugging and talking. The aubergine turned to Sweet P and Pumpkin.

'I am Aliya,' said the friend. 'I too am from Syria. I am very happy to see my friend again.'

'We'll drive you both to the camp,' said Sweet P.

'Thank you, but we will walk. It is not so far. And I must wait here for my sister.'

They all stood for a while looking at each other before hugging goodbye. It felt so sad. They had just made a new friend and now they had to leave her.

'Thank you for helping me. You are very kind,' said Amina.

'Good luck!' said Pumpkin.

'One day we will try to find you,' said Sweet P. 'Look out for the big red van!'

They drove away slowly, waving through the open windows.

'So Aliya is a refugee too,' said Sweet P.

'Oh dear, I hope they will be all right,' said Pumpkin.

'Me too. It all feels wrong,' said Sweet P sadly.

They had found so many things on their journey, but today they had found a stowaway, though really Amina had found them.

# – CHAPTER SIXTEEN –
## WILL THEY MAKE IT?

*Greek Words:*
*Parakaló = p-a-r-a-k-a-l-OA* = please
*Eínai éna megálo próvlima = EE-n-ai E-n-a m-e-g-A-l-oa p-r-O-v-l-i-m-a* = It's a big problem
*Eínai makriá = EE-n-ai m-a-k-r-ee-A* = It's far
*Poté = p-o-t-AI*= never
*Kalí týchi! = k-a-l-EE t-I-ch-i* = Good luck! *(Remember that ch again – bad throat!)*
*Tavérnes = t-a-v-AIR-n-e-s* = taverns, cafés

Pumpkin and Sweet P walked along the pretty harbour to the tourist office. On arrival they were given a map and guidebook of Lesvos by a helpful zucchini with short spiky hair, just like Sweet P's. She spoke good English.

'We have a very beautiful island, *korítsia*. What are you looking for? Good beach, a small town, or a bigger one with many hotels?'

'Oh, we definitely want a good beach,' said Sweet P, 'and not too big a town. We have our own van to sleep in, so we don't need a hotel.'

'A small place with travellers as well as locals, artists and folk like us?' asked Pumpkin, hopefully.

*And a bit like you too!* thought Sweet P, smiling knowingly.

'Ah, I know just the place. Skala Eressos where many like-minded folk go. Look on this map. It is famous for the poet Sappho who lived there a long time ago. She wrote beautiful words, and we still read them today. It is a special village and very charming.'

'That's it then eh, Pumps?'

'Sounds perfect!'

*'Efcharistó!'* said Sweet P.

*'Polý!'* said Pumpkin, 'and for the map.'

'And for the guidebook!' said Sweet P.

Folk were sat in the *tavérnes*, having their breakfast, chatting in the early morning sunshine. It seemed a very cheery place. Back in *Van Rouge*, Pumpkin and Sweet P studied the map and set off across Lesvos to Skala Eressos in the south west of the island.

'I can't believe we'll soon be at the end of our journey, Sweet P!'

'The trip meter says we've driven one thousand six hundred and forty-five miles since we left West Wales!' said Sweet P, patting the dashboard to thank *Van Rouge* for bringing them so far.

'And only fifty-five to go!' said Pumpkin.

*Now what's that in kilometres?* mused Sweet P.

They left the outskirts of Mytiline behind and drove along the shore of the Gulf of Yera.

'So that's about two thousand seven hundred and thirty-five kilometres in all!' announced Sweet P. She liked adding up numbers in her head. Pumpkin looked at her in disbelief.

As the road climbed into a pine forest, they glimpsed at the blue of the Gulf of Kaloní ahead through the trees. They drove down the long hill and soon came to the saltpans.

'Just look at all those pink flamingos, Sweet P!' Pumpkin prided herself on her bird knowledge.

'And that huge pile of salt, Pumpkin.'

There were many red poppies and wild flowers growing as well as red, pink and white oleanders planted along the roadside. After the town of Kaloní the road went right along the shore of the Gulf for a while. They stopped at one of the small beaches, let Hen out for a stretch and put some water out for her. A wizened, kindly-looking olive was dozing on an old bench under a tree, so they walked quietly into the water. It was shallow for a long way, but once they had waded out, they had a lovely swim.

'Look, there's a shower over there,' said Pumpkin.

They hadn't had a shower since they left Wales. It consisted of a bent pipe with a shower rose on the end, set in concrete in the sand. They turned it on and a trickle of warm water came out.

'Hmm, not that impressive!' said Sweet P laughing.

They squeezed and hung their swimming gear on the washing pole. Hen did not want to hop back in her basket, and they ended up chasing her up and down the beach. The poor olive awoke with a fright and looked disgruntled.

Hen was running frantically around. 'Let's throw the sack over Hen. It worked the other day!' said Sweet P.

'Good plan!'

Sweet P eventually threw the sack over Hen and she became instantly still. Pumpkin grabbed her and popped her into the basket. Pumpkin and Sweet P now felt hot again and had another swim to cool down.

'You know, I'm becoming quite fond of Hen. What about you, Pumps?' (Long pause.)

'I am too actually, just as long as she doesn't nip me again!'

*

Back on the road, *Van Rouge* started to climb once more, with fantastic views of the glittering blue water of the Gulf they were leaving behind.

'Hey, that's the horseshoe shape we saw on the map, Pumps.'

There were short shrubby trees, olive trees, and more oleanders popping up by the roadside.

'Pull over here. I'm going to pick some, Sweet P!' Pumpkin gathered a few red and white oleanders and put them in the tin (with water) by the small sky windscreen. She took over driving. They started to climb a long hill.

'Uh oh, I can hear a bad noise, Pumps, can you? The engine sounds all wrong!'

'Hmm, not really...' They drove a bit further and higher. 'Oh, you're right, it sounds terrible!'

They stopped, kept the engine running and lifted the bonnet. There was definitely a banging sound and it was loud.

'Oh dear, sounds like the engine. We're over half way. I suppose we'll just have to keep going and keep our fingers crossed,' said Sweet P.

Just then she spotted something lying by the side of the road. It was a gourd, just like the ones they had seen painted and swinging gaily under the pergola in Kostas' *tavérna*.

'How strange to find this here. Lucky it wasn't

run over. I wonder if someone dropped it or it fell out of something. I'll paint it and hang it up later.' Pumpkin was slightly miffed that she hadn't seen it first; she was the finder on this journey after all.

Back on the road, the noise was still there. In fact it now sounded much worse, especially as they drove uphill. There were few roads crossing the island, so at least they shouldn't get lost. They took the lower of the two routes that crosses Lesvos from the southeast to the southwest.

'Just as well we didn't take the mountain road. I don't think *Van Rouge* could have taken all the ups and downs!' said Sweet P.

They staggered up another steep hill, barely daring to breathe as they coaxed *Van Rouge* all the way to the top.

'Phew, now we can roll down,' said Pumpkin, 'and look there's a garage at the bottom, Sweet P!'

They banged and clattered onto the garage forecourt. An old zucchini ran out looking horrified.

'*Geia sas*! *Parakaló*, we have a problem. Please can you look at our van?' said Sweet P smiling, anxious and hopeful all at the same time.

'*Eínai éna megálo próvlima korítsia!* Where you come from?'

'From *Oualía*!' said Sweet P.

'*Ochi!* In this old van, *poté! Eínai makriá!*'

'Yes, it is a very long way. Do you know what the problem might be?' asked Pumpkin, biting her tongue.

'*Megálo próvlima!* It is the engine. You must go to Mytilíni or Kaloní, to a big garage.'

'We've just come from there! We're going to Skala Eressos. Will we make it?' asked Sweet P.

'Hmmm. *Kalí týchi, korítsia!*' He turned away shaking his head.

'I think that means good luck, but he did not look like he thought we'd have it!' said Pumpkin.

Things did not look good. Despite this, they set off, slightly dejected with Pumpkin more than happy to let Sweet P drive again and deal with a sick *Van Rouge.*

*Surely we won't break down now with only a few kilometres to go? All we can do is carry on and hope for the best,* thought Pumpkin.

They climbed up and coasted down a few more steep hills. As they went further inland, they found themselves in a lunar-like landscape of bare arid hills and strangely-shaped rocks. According to the guidebook, Lesvos was a volcanic island and molten rock (lava) had made these funny shapes a very long time ago.

A few miles further on, they were looking down onto a big expanse of sparkling water in the distance. 'Hey, I can see the Aegean sea!' cried Sweet P. On the horizon loomed a mountainous island, ethereal in the heat haze.

'That must be *Chíos*,' said Pumpkin, checking the map. 'We were there early this morning!'

Down below them was a lush valley, a green patch amongst the bare rock, the only real green they had seen since leaving the pine trees near Mytilíni. They rolled down the hills, struggled up them, silvery olive trees waving in the breeze.

'We've seen a lot of olive trees today. It says here that Lesvos is known As 'The Olive Island', said Pumpkin.

Sweet P was absorbed in the bangs, clatters and clangs. 'Yes, it's got to be the engine,' she said, glumly.

They caught the occasional glimpse of tiny boats on the distant sea and before long they came to a T junction. It was right to Eressos and left to Skala Eressos (Σκάλα Ερεσού in Greek writing).

They turned left and bumped and banged down the long straight road, until they came to a bridge which they could either go over or take a right.

'This way goes to the beach,' said Pumpkin,

looking up from the map and pointing to the right. 'We don't want to breakdown and get stuck in the town!'

'Good idea,' said Sweet P, turning.

'And right here!' said Pumpkin as they came parallel to the sea. Sweet P turned left towards the sea down the sandy track (Pumpkin had got muddled again). She drove very slowly to the end where there were a few shady trees, with the sea and beach beyond. She parked sideways under the biggest tamarisk tree and switched off the noisy engine.

'Phew, we've made it, Pumps, even if we get no further!'

They high fived, had a big hug and jumped out of *Van Rouge*. They ran onto a long sandy beach with a big rocky headland at one end. It was greyish sand but beautiful, and the sparkling blue sea looked very inviting. To the left, way along the beach was a cluster of houses around a small hill with a ruin at the top. In front of it was a row of *tavérnes* along the sea. Out to sea there was a big rock.

'That must be Skala Eressos!' called Pumpkin, looking through the binoculars. 'Those *tavérnas* are all built on stilts!'

They let Hen out of her basket and gave her a bowl of water and she clucked contentedly as she strutted around. She explored the new spot before flopping on her side to sunbathe, wings askew.

'This is perfect. Swim?' asked Sweet P, grinning.

'You bet!' Pumpkin was already hopping across the hot sand. They threw themselves into the sea and leaped and splashed around in sheer joy. They were swimming in the Aegean Sea.

After a long while they wandered back to *Van Rouge*. They ate some crackers, feta cheese and cherries, threw some bits to Hen and devised a plan. A tabby cat appeared, followed by a white and black cat, both going for Hen's food. Hen squawked, flapped and hopped, and the cats scarpered.

'We've arrived at our Greek island, Pumps. Just like we planned. Maybe *Van Rouge* has had enough. If we're very lucky, we can drive or be towed to the tiny patch of land,' said Sweet P.

'We have to find it first!' said Pumpkin. 'We need to let the good folk of Skala Eressos know what we're looking for. Let's see if we can find a big piece of wood on the beach to make a sign.'

They explored the long beach, diving in for a swim whenever they needed to cool off.

'Weeeeee!' called Sweet P as she came up from a handstand.

'Hooweee!' cried Pumpkin, holding up a sizeable driftwood plank she had found.

They set up their chairs under the trees, fixed the table with the broken leg. Over a nice cup of tea they discussed what to put on the sign in big letters.

'I'm a messy writer, Pumps. You'd better do the sign. You're bound to be neater than me.'

'I am rather good at writing!' said Pumpkin, picking up her fat pen.

```
WANTED

GOOD HOME 4 OLD VAN & 2
FINE RESIDENTS & HEN
IN XCHANGE FOR FOLLOWING SERVICES:
   * FIDDLER — TUNES FOR ANY OCCASION *
   * JUGGLER EXTRAORDINAIRE *
   * DANCING IN TUTUS *
   * DUSTING  OPTIONAL TUTUS *
   * TRAFFIC DIRECTING *
   * GARDENING *
   *   EGGS *
```

# THE END - FOR NOW!

PS. A fiddle is a violin. The one with the red dot on her nose is a clown.

I would like to give special thanks to you children and your parents for pre-ordering this book. Without your support it would have taken me a lot longer to get it out into the world. THANK YOU! I hope you really enjoyed the adventure . Do let me know!

Ana Sophie Rijkhoff
Anabel & Oscar Weeks
Asha & Kel Kahindi
Bear Francis
Bertie & Ivy Read
Caleb & Layla Issa
Charlie Norman
Daisy, Bertie & Bonnie Maiden
Dean O'Reilly
Elsie Bean Webley
Elsie Dougherty
Emily & Edward Davies
Enola, Ella & Cree Wilbraham
Enya Chivers
Freya & Wilfred Foley
Graham Elaine
Harri & Alys Davies
Hefin & Deri Wild
Isaac Allen
Isla & Eva Caird
Isla Jo Robertson
Iwan & Rhys Evans
Jackson Jorden
Jess Davies
Joshua & Athena Widdowson

Kaya Labonte-Hurst
Kita Squires
Leila Haf Jones
Leo and Asher Turgel
Lily & Cei Squires
Lucas Timothy & Naia Nerys Walker Arroyo
Matilda Yannaghas
Merlin, Alice & Marylou Klein
Milly & Jac Thompson-Attrill
Myla & Ronny Waller
Myrtle Keane
Norah & Alex Desreaux
Olivia Dunnell
Oscar & Noah Ralph
Otto & Albi Harper Cooling
Rowan Christopher
Ruby Florence Greenfield-Smith
Simon and Callum Davies
Sophia Marshall
Sophie Poot Harries
Sylvie, Leon & Ethan Daley
Taliesin Telerin Lane & Seren Irina Haywood
Theodore Thomas
Toby Daniel Stretton
Ty Norman Dobson
William Lyndon Blank
Zach Price